# The Sheikh's For

CW00701737

## Mel Tesl

# Chapter One

Yasmine Al-Fasih slipped like a wraith into the bedroom suite that had been prepared for her father's esteemed and honored guest, Sheikh Jamal Qadir.

Her eyes narrowed as she glanced around the suitably luxurious accommodation with its sitting room, sunken bedroom with huge circular bed, the adjoining theatre room and bathroom with plunge pool. The only thing missing was a kitchen, but no guest was expected to cook when there were Michelin five star chefs on hand to create the finest dining at any hour of the day or night.

That her father kept five overpaid chefs never ceased to amaze her. It was so unnecessary when their economy had taken a huge nosedive these last three years. Even parts of the palace were bordering on rack and ruin.

But despite the fact they were an oil-dry country, her father liked to pretend they were one of the wealthiest countries in the Middle East. A pity he'd relied on the now failing tourism for far too long. He hadn't diversified and she wondered if he'd left it too little too late, and that perhaps even negotiations with Sheikh Jamal wouldn't save them.

She paused at the top of the trio of steps that led to the huge bed and its occupant, whose potent rose petal fragrance filled her nostrils. Yasmine wasn't surprised to find her dad's favorite concubine, Shakira, lying in wait for their visitor. Nothing less than the best was expected for Jamal, Sheikh of Ishmat.

His pleasure and happiness was paramount.

Although many of the old-school sheikhs didn't allow the women of their harem to be shared around, it was becoming quite the fashion for the modern sheikhs of some countries to enjoy the status and bragging rights that came with giving esteemed guests a favorite harem woman for a night. Particularly if they wanted a favor in return like her father did from Sheikh Jamal.

She swallowed hard as all her hard won confidence drained away. How could she possibly measure up to someone of Shakira's seductive looks and experience in the bedroom? Yasmine might be considered a beauty and royalty to boot, but she was as shackled by tradition—it was forbidden for a man to touch a sheikha—as surely as her father's harem women were by their looks and their sexual duties.

Yasmine's dad, Sheikh Zameer Al-Fasih, went to great measures for those men who were more powerful than him. That included the beastly Sheikh Arif Hakim, whom her father had ordered Yasmine to marry in a little over three weeks. That Sheikh Arif was older than her father and twice as cruel left her insides weak and her throat raw.

She refused to marry him!

The thought propelled her forward once again. She took the trio of steps, her nose wrinkling as she inhaled the overpowering rose petal scent, hiding her distaste at seeing Shakira lying on the bed in a seductive pose and a sultry smile, one that disappeared the moment she saw Yasmine.

Shakira sat up, her dark eyes flashing and her full lips twisting into a pout. "What are you doing here? I was expecting Sheikh Jamal."

"Sorry to disappoint you," Yasmine refuted coolly. "But your services aren't required tonight. You may go."

Shakira's full breasts quivered through her gauzy top. "Says who?"

*Says me.*

"What does it matter?" Yasmine wasn't above using her superior voice to get things done. The last thing she wanted was for Sheikh Jamal to arrive before Shakira had obeyed her marching orders. "Your replacement has already been decided."

"Replacement?" Shakira threw her mass of dark hair over one shoulder, her eyes that were lined heavily with kohl blinking suspiciously. "I'm your father's favorite. He gives me to all his important friends."

Yasmine hid a grimace. It turned her stomach that these harem women wanted to service other men. That her dad regularly visited his harem while his wife, Valentina—Yasmine's English mother—was expected to stay faithful, was even worse. Her mother was miserable and it made Yasmine resent her dad's other lovers even more.

It was an effort just to stay civil. "Yet my dad keeps my mother all to himself. What does that tell you?"

Shakira's eyes flashed, her envy of Sheikha Valentina all too clear. "I'll be speaking to Sheikh Zameer about this!"

"Go ahead. Though you'll have to make your complaint in the morning." At Shakira's ugly frown, Yasmine added, "My dad is spending the night with my mother."

*Liar.* Her father rarely spent any night with her mother these days. But it wasn't like it never happened. The occasion was just becoming less and less frequent.

But hopefully Yasmine's bluff would work and give her all the time she needed to seduce Sheikh Jamal and force his hand in marriage. She couldn't suffer a miserable existence with the old goat, Arif. Being married to him would be even worse than what her mom endured with her dad.

Although chaining Sheikh Jamal to Yasmine for life would see him hate her, at least he wouldn't deliberately hurt her. She'd done her research. He wasn't cruel. He was known for his fairness. But he wasn't a pushover, either. He was merciless when needed. She sighed. She would just have to learn to live with his resentment and whatever justice he might mete out.

"Why are you here?" Shakira asked. "You're not the usual messenger girl."

Yasmine glowered. No other harem girl would question the daughter of their sheikh. Though Yasmine didn't class herself as a sheikha, the title belonged to her. It was past time she remembered it. "Go. Now. Or I'll be the one to speak to my father first thing in the morning."

"Fine," Shakira muttered. She climbed off the bed in a cloud of sickening floral perfume and billowy, ethereal fabric, then stalked up the steps and out of the bedroom suite, her bare feet making no sound.

Yasmine exhaled slowly as the door clicked shut, her stomach tightening with a fresh batch of terror that threatened to change her mind. *No.* It was now or never. If she left now and yielded to her dad's command to marry old Sheikh Arif she'd be subjected to a life of tyranny and cruelty. If she stayed and seduced the famed Sheikh Jamal, at least she wouldn't suffer a lifetime of abuse.

Would she?

*No.* She bit her bottom lip. Whatever punishment Sheikh Jamal devised it'd still be a thousand times better than living with an ancient despot. She'd throw herself at Jamal's mercy any day over being abused and mistreated by an old goat famous for his shameless depravity and ugliness inside and out.

She might never have met Jamal but she'd done enough research on him and uncovered many photos. He was stupidly handsome. Little wonder women fell at his feet. His half-brother, who lived in another palace, was gorgeous too. She was only surprised both of them weren't already married.

She took off her jeweled sandals. Though it'd be nice to find love, she could live without it. She didn't have a choice. She'd managed fine for twenty years in the lack of affection from men, what was another half-century or so?

Lifting her hands she pulled free her keffiyeh and shook out her blonde hair—a color inherited from her English mother—then slipped off her abaya to reveal her gauzy harem outfit beneath. It'd been easy enough to steal. The hard part would be losing her virginity to a stranger.

She sighed. She'd be twenty-one in a few months and she'd yet to know the touch of a lover. It left her a little queasy and lightheaded knowing it was her first time and she had no real idea what to expect, other than being aware it would hurt.

*Don't even think about it. You're doing what needs to be done for a better future.*

She lay on the bed and positioned herself in the same way Shakira had been. She grimaced. How the hell was this comfortable? She gave up and lay on her side. The moment Jamal arrived she'd move back into the same seductive pose Shakira had done so well.

Settling onto the bed, she lay quietly. The silence ticked by and she sighed luxuriously at the soft pillow and mattress. A cloud couldn't be more comfortable. She closed her eyes momentarily. Jamal might be hours yet.

She promptly fell asleep.

\*

Sheikh Jamal Qadir followed the male servant who escorted him to his bedroom suite. Though the palace was pure luxury, he couldn't help but note how the expensive furnishings were fading and a little tattered in some rooms, the beautiful pieces dusty and unpolished.

It was clear that Sheikh Zameer's once impressive wealth was fading, too. But then tourism had been brought to a standstill for the whole world of late, not just for those countries in the Middle East. Little wonder the sheikh was so eager to begin trading with Jamal.

After a few right and then left turns along wide corridors, the servant swung open a door and stepped aside. Jamal nodded thanks and walked into the suite, the servant then shutting the door with a *snick.* Jamal ignored his surroundings and headed straight toward the bathroom.

Thank heavens this was a short stay, no more than an overnight visit. He was already over the scraping and bowing of Zameer's servants. He pulled off his robe as he glanced at the plunge pool. It looked inviting, but then so did the double-headed shower. At least his rooms were adequate, with little expense spared.

His host, Sheikh Zameer, clearly kept some suites up-to-date to impress his visitors.

Jamal stepped into the shower and lifted his face into the hot water. His advisors had already informed him that Zameer's finances had been stagnating for quite some time. Though Amack was still considered a wealthy nation thanks to its pristine mountain ranges surrounded by endless desert and sandy dunes, which made it the bucket list of many tourists, the travel industry was fading fast.

Tourism had all but shuddered to a stop. Add Sheikh Zameer's old fashioned ideals that hadn't progressed his country forward and its people would soon be in real financial trouble.

Jamal lathered his hair and skin, then rinsed off the suds before he turned off the water and stepped out to dry off. Although his own country produced good quality dates, buying a whole lot more from the date-laden Amack while helping to keep the country afloat until tourism resumed—and even beyond that—would not only keep their nations at peace, he'd be able to export date liquor all over the world thanks to his handful of distilleries.

In exchange he'd live with selling oil to his neighbor for a lower price. Jamal would still make a profit. It was a win-win. Not that he needed the boost to his own economy. He had his thumb in enough pies to continue flooding Ishmat with wealth. But only a fool would reject more influx of cash, and it wouldn't hurt to add to his already prolific portfolio.

At thirty-two years of age he was already one of the richest men on the planet, right along with his half-brother and closest friends. They really did all have the Midas touch.

The only trouble with wealth and power were those who coveted it from him. It was only lucky he had a powerful alliance with his friends and half-brother, which safeguarded one another and deterred potential conflict.

Placing the towel back onto its heated rack, he walked naked out of the bathroom. Tiredness was pulling at him every which way. It had been a long day. Sleep was in order.

He froze on the top step that led to the sunken bedroom and its inviting bed.

Weariness slipped off him as heat rushed through his blood and he stared at the blonde angel waiting for him. That she was sound asleep mattered little to him. It highlighted an innocent quality that shouldn't be apparent being that she must be one of Zameer's harem girls.

It was now patently clear Zameer wasn't totally old fashioned if he was willing to share one of his harem girls.

Jamal's dick jerked and thickened, and he swallowed past his suddenly dry throat. She was exquisite. The blonde bombshell must surely be Zameer's favorite lover.

He stalked down the steps, a growl forming in his throat. He didn't make a habit of mixing business with pleasure. But he wasn't a fool either, he'd had a productive day, and tonight he'd enjoy his reward.

# Chapter Two

Yasmine moaned at the kisses pressed to her throat, her blood warming, thrumming, her nerve endings rejoicing at the seductive touch that awakened needs she hadn't even known she had.

*Best. Dream. Ever.*

If this was what she might expect from Jamal for her first ever sexual encounter then she'd be deliriously happy, because once he found out her ploy she doubted she'd ever enjoy hot sex with him again. He'd be too busy hating on her and giving her the cold shoulder.

In the meantime this dream would have to suffice. That it wasn't real mattered little, she'd go with the flow and enjoy every second of her vivid imagination.

Her dream lover deftly removed her clothes, air touching her exposed body while his rumble of appreciation sent needy shivers down her spine. His hands ran up and down her torso, leaving goose bumps in their wake, his mouth closing over the tip of one breast before his tongue laved the hard peak of her nipple.

Sparks ignited and heat escalated, and she arched her back with a sigh of pleasure as electricity danced through her and centered at her core. She almost wished she was a harem girl herself if this was how sex affected her.

He released her breast and she squirmed, aching at the loss of contact. His dark chuckle reverberated through her—so tangible she'd swear it was real—then his hot mouth closed over her other breast, her untrained body reveling in the exquisite sensation of his mouth, hands and tongue on her.

"So incredibly beautiful and responsive."

Her senses screamed with awareness and her eyes jerked open. *Shit.* She hadn't been dreaming! Sheikh Jamal looked down at her with a satisfied smile and heated eyes, his gorgeous body as naked as her own.

But though she was drawn to his seductive touch and looks, it was instinctive to stiffen with rejection while words of rebuffal formed. How dare he imagine for one second he could lay a finger on her!

*This is what you want, remember?*

Jamal's eyes hardened fractionally. "It's a bit too late now for second thoughts, angel. And though you might be here for my pleasure, I'll make sure your pleasure is great, too."

She swallowed hard. *Oh, crap.* Was she ready for this? She might have had a few years in England to broaden her horizons and finish her business and modern languages degree but she'd never be uninhibited like so many western women. Paradoxically, while she'd found some of them crass and too easy with their charms, they'd accused of being an ice queen.

If only they'd known how close to the truth they'd been. She'd never revealed she was a sheikha, yet everyone had labelled her as royalty—even if it'd been of the superficial kind.

She managed a smile that she hoped was sexy. "Then what are you waiting for Sheikh Jamal?"

His gaze sparked, and he reached for her nearest hand to place it on his steel-hard shaft. She automatically clasped him, her pulse accelerating at his long, satiny smoothness. That he was so damn big left her breathless and a little dizzy. How would he even fit inside her? She hid a betraying gulp and instead moved her hand experimentally up and down his length.

His breath shuddered out, his lashes sweeping low and concealing his thoughts. She had no clue what she was doing but guessed she was doing something right. His clenched jaw and taut shoulders said he was already on the edge. That he was gratified by her simple touch boosted her confidence.

"Do you like that?" she asked huskily, increasing the speed of her strokes before he clamped hold of her hand to still her.

"Keep doing that and I'll spill my seed before I'm even inside you."

Shockwaves of delight pulsed through her. She supposed that was a *yes*, then.

His dark, gleaming eyes held hers. "And I'm sure neither one of us wants that. I want you screaming out my name as we come together."

He bent and kissed her even as she stiffened at the dawning realization she was risking more than her reputation by having sex with him. What had she been thinking? She wasn't on birth control like many harem girls were.

Before she could voice objection, he aligned his cock between her legs and thrust his length deep inside her.

She cried out at the red-hot, searing burn, her inner muscles stretched so far beyond capability, the pain took away all thought or comprehension.

Jamal stilled and sucked in a shocked breath. "What the hell?"

He stared down at her for a beat, a savage curse spilling from his lips just as the bedroom suite door crashed open.

Her father stood inside the doorway. His face blanched as he visibly recoiled at the scene below him. "Yasmine! What is this?" he roared.

It was an outer body experience to look at the man she was somehow related to by blood. Sometimes she wondered how it was possible when they were so very different. That she was numb to everything, including his rage, had to be a good thing. "What does it look like, Dad?"

"*Dad?*" Jamal echoed, his features drawing tight. Sucking in a pained breath, he withdrew from her and stood shamelessly nude beside the bed, his cock as hard as a pike and his face even harder. He might have been some fearless pagan God facing a coming battle.

Yasmine grimaced at their separation that wasn't just a physical loss. Despite them being little more than strangers, the loss between them was emotional, too. It took everything she had not to reach for him and instead cover her body with a blanket.

That she felt little better than pond scum when Shakira moved to stand behind Yasmine's father like *she* was the queen of the flaming realm only exacerbated everything a hundred fold.

Clearly Shakira hadn't believed Zameer was staying the night with Yasmine's mother.

If that wasn't enough to set Yasmine's blood to boil, Shakira staring at Jamal's cock with a slow and provocative lick of her lips sent a flare of rage through Yasmine right along with a little envy. She'd never know now what real sex felt like. Not after this delightful little escapade. Jamal wouldn't go near her.

It might yet be Shakira who slaked his lust.

*Not if I have any say in it.*

Her father stomped down the stairs, a nerve throbbing to life in his jaw and all his attention fixated on his daughter. "Did you forget about your wedding to Sheikh Arif in three weeks' time?" he roared. "You've wrecked everything! How do you propose I save our country now from short-term financial ruin?"

Her vision clouded and her pulse pounded in her ears. She should have known her upcoming nuptials weren't just about peace negotiations. Her father was getting financial assistance from her future husband. She was little more than a broodmare.

But then when had her happiness ever mattered to her father?

"I don't know, Dad. Do you have any other daughters you can sell to the highest bidder?"

Her dad lifted his hand, his palm hitting her face with a loud, stinging *crack.*

Tears welled but she didn't cry. She didn't back down. This was her one chance to be honest. "You hate that I wasn't the son you wanted, don't you?"

He bristled. "Your western blood doesn't give you the right to disrespect me and act how you please." He shook his head. "I should never have impregnated your mother. Yes, I wanted a son and you've been nothing but—"

"That's enough."

Jamal's voice might be quiet and controlled, but it throbbed with undercurrents of menace. "Your daughter is willful and strong, traits you might admire in a man."

"Except she's not a man!" her dad refuted.

"No. She's a beautiful, independent woman. One I can't help but admire. As should you."

Yasmine's heart soared that Jamal defended her. She'd expected fury, not compassion.

Her father refocused on Jamal, and Yasmine could almost see the gears shifting in his crafty mind. "And just how far does that admiration go? Are you willing to marry her?"

Jamal crossed his arms and cocked a brow, and Yasmine held her breath. Her entire future hinged on his answer. That he was a renowned playboy, a bachelor who loved his single life, meant marrying her wouldn't be advantageous to him. He was beyond sexy and filthy rich; he could have any woman he wanted.

"The way I see it you don't have a choice," her father added. "You've ruined her for Sheikh Arif. He wanted a virgin bride."

Her dad was pushing too hard, damn it. She only hoped Jamal's strong moral code would see him do the right thing.

"Of course that does come with certain...stipulations," her father added.

Yasmine clenched her hands. Her dad needed to shut up before Jamal went running for the hills.

"Like a big, fat dowry?" Jamal asked drily.

"It only seems fair," her father said, adjusting the double cord of his agal that kept his ghutrah in place on his head.

Yasmine knew the habit well. Her dad was nervous. He really must have a lot on the line by marrying off his only legitimate daughter.

Jamal nodded. "Very well."

She turned to Jamal. "Wait. You *want* to marry me?" she asked in a croaky voice, her face heating as she glanced at his powerful physique, his impressive manhood.

"Don't sound so surprised," he said mildly. "It's the honorable thing to do." He shrugged. "And I'm certain you will give me many sons and daughters."

"Children?" she said weakly. Is that all she was to any man—a broodmare?

"Isn't that what you want from me in return?" Jamal asked.

She glanced at her dad. His fuchsia-flushed face had already faded back to its normal swarthy color. In fact, he looked rather pleased by the outcome. Of course her dad would be happy. Not only would he get grandchildren he'd get a filthy-rich son-in-law into the bargain...a sheikh, no less.

"I—"

"Jamal might already have planted his seed inside you," her dad interjected.

"Unlikely," Jamal said, his shrewd eyes swinging back and forth between father and daughter. "We didn't get that far."

Her father exhaled and pointed to the splotch of blood on the sheets. "I think it's fair to say you went far enough." He rubbed his hands together. "We'll bring the wedding forward. I'm sure Sheikh Arif will understand."

"I'm sure he will," Jamal acknowledged with a dry smile. "As much as he covets my lands I have far more wealth than he does, not to mention powerful allies. That he will now also covet my soon-to-be wife will be just another thorn in his side he will have to learn to live with."

"Then it's decided. Welcome to the family, Sheikh Jamal Qadir," her father announced loudly, proffering his hand. "I look forward to a whole posse of grandsons."

Jamal held Yasmine's gaze. "And at least one daughter who looks just like her mother."

She resisted stamping her feet and shouting there was more to her than a fertile womb. Instead she pasted a smile on her face. *Be careful what you wish for.* She had a sudden feeling things wouldn't go her way quite as easily from here on in.

# Chapter Three

Jamal resisted an urge to stride—*sprint!*—out of the bedroom suite and away from the woman who'd just trapped him into joining her family. *Fuck.* What had possessed him to give in so easily? Was it the disturbing slap Yasmine's father had delivered to his daughter?

Jamal abhorred violence against women.

He'd seen enough of that with his father and the mistreatment of his two wives. The only good thing to have come out of his dad's second marriage was Jamal's half-brother, Dhamar. Not that they saw each other often these days, with their mothers having to be separated into different palaces to keep the peace.

Since their father's death three years ago from a boating accident, Jamal had taken on leadership of Ishmat while Dhamar had been busy running his mother's native homeland of Chawait. His lips twisted. What would Dhamar say when he found out his older, playboy brother was getting married?

Jamal was going to have to make some adjustments. Not only would he need to extend his stay here in Amack to announce his engagement and its accompanying celebrations, he'd need to make arrangements for their wedding at Ishmat.

*Don't forget about the ballroom you'll need to build.*

He smiled. Hamid, one of his best friends, had made a bet with Jamal and their two other close sheikh friends, Mahindar and Fayez, that if any of them fell in love and married they'd build a grand ballroom to celebrate the event. They'd all stupidly agreed.

It seemed no sooner had Hamid's suggestion been put out into the universe, it had come after each of them, one at a time.

15

Fayez was next. Though no one doubted for a second he was already halfway in love with his mistress, Jazmina. How long it'd take before Fayez would admit it was another thing entirely.

Jamal smiled grimly. He had enough on his plate without worrying about Fayez. He had no doubt his future wife would keep him on his toes.

His dick twitched, and he stifled a curse at the aching heaviness of his balls. He owed it to Yasmine to marry her. That she'd been a virgin meant he had no other choice but to do the right thing by her. Only a man without honor, scruples or pride would do otherwise.

That she'd tricked him into marriage gave every indication that *she* had no honor, scruples or pride. But a part of him didn't blame her. They lived in a man's world, at least in his culture—his western education had shown him that. And as a sheikha Yasmine would have even less rights.

If he'd been in her shoes having to marry Sheikh Arif, he too would have been desperate enough to find a way out of it. The man was a pig. That Yasmine's father had been prepared to hand her over to a known despot spoke volumes about the kind of person Jamal was about to do trade with.

If it wasn't that he'd soon be marrying Zameer's daughter he'd think twice about their trade deal now. It was why he'd never had business relations with Arif. The man was a monster, and Zameer clearly wasn't a whole lot better to give his only daughter to Arif in the name of financial security.

"Get dressed," Zameer snapped to his daughter. "You'll be sleeping under lock and key tonight and every night until your marriage."

As her dad went to spin around and return to the woman waiting in the doorway with sharp eyes and too much makeup, Jamal reached out and clapped his hand around the older man's wrist. Only when Zameer turned wide, disbelieving eyes toward him, did Jamal state calmly, "I expect Yasmine to be treated with the respect she deserves as a sheikha and my soon-to-be wife. Is that clear?"

Zameer's nostrils flared and his lips flattened. He was obviously not used to someone else issuing commands. But though defiance was briefly stamped onto every hard line of his face, he released a long, low sigh and slumped. "Of course."

That color rose in Yasmine's cheeks, her posture stiff and unyielding, and her cornflower blue eyes wide, revealed much about her past and present. But then she'd likely dealt with her father's abuse many times.

It was beyond Jamal's comprehension why that left his heartbeat pounding and his ears roaring. All he knew for sure was that he'd protect Yasmine, now and in the future, with everything he had. Focusing on Zameer, he stated quietly, "No one touches her from now on except me."

There was no mistaking the undercurrents of malice and warning in his voice, and Zameer took a jerky step back the moment Jamal released his wrist.

Zameer nodded. "You have my word."

Jamal managed a tight smile. "Good." Then he turned to his future wife, reached for her hand, and raised it to his lips. "I'll see you soon, angel."

# Chapter Four

Yasmine was left speechless as her future husband kissed her knuckles, electricity zinging through her while his dark eyes held hers. She swallowed hard. She'd never expected him to be gallant. That he'd protected her from any further punishment from her father left her reeling.

She'd expected nothing less than Jamal's scorn.

A shiver went through her. That this kind, perhaps even devoted man would soon be her husband, made hope beat wildly in her chest.

She managed to smile at him before she scooped up her abaya and wrapped the blanket tighter around her. Then she climbed the steps and disappeared into the bathroom to get dressed.

She closed the door behind her and took a deep breath of the sandalwood soap scent that still lingered in the air. Jamal had obviously taken a shower, and her mind immediately conjured up visions of his nude, wet and lathered body. A deep quiver started in her belly as she recalled his hard body, his even harder cock.

The quiver took on a life of its own at the realization he really was going to be her husband, and that all her planning had come to fruition.

That she was no longer a virgin meant little to her. Yes, he'd penetrated her and caused her hymen to break, but they hadn't really had sex and she was yet to know the full effects of how her body reacted to his. Even if he'd only be with her to create children, she was glad the pain of being a virgin was behind her now and that the next time she might fully enjoy sex with him.

She pulled the abaya over her head and allowed the loose, dark fabric to fall to her ankles, effectively covering her up. How would Sheikh Arif react when he heard the news she was no longer going to be his wife? She bit her bottom lip. She only hoped he didn't start a war with Jamal.

*Doubtful.* Not only was Jamal powerful and rich, with powerful and rich allies, he had a half-brother whose wealth was considered excessive, even by Arab standards.

Her dad was waiting for her—of course he was, she was priceless to him now—and after he nodded at Jamal, he escorted her out of the guest room and into the corridor.

Yasmine felt Jamal's gaze on her the whole way but refused to look at him. She was still digesting the fact her plan had worked. Was still figuring out how she felt about that—about Jamal!

Her dad walked beside her without a word, his face hiding his thoughts. Despite her rocky relationship with her father, guilt for a moment surged. "Dad, I know you might not approve of what I did, but—"

"Approve?" he chuckled hoarsely. "You've become more like me than I realized. You got Jamal good, didn't you?"

Her breath caught in her too-thick throat. "It wasn't like that, Dad. I didn't have a choice."

"You looked for another solution. I couldn't have planned it better myself! I'd never even considered Jamal as I didn't for a second imagine he'd be the type to want marriage."

If she was meant to feel proud because of her dad's praise, she felt anything but. She felt...sick. Like she was becoming her father. Like his dirty laundry had stained hers.

"I only hope Jamal will forgive me."

"Forgive you?" He snorted. "He's besotted by you. If you play your cards right he'll give you the world." His glinting eyes swept over her.

"Just don't forget where you came from and that your people here need you."

A kick in the face couldn't have hurt more. Her father was using her as a cash cow, even before the marriage certificate had been signed. That he was already getting a substantial dowry from Jamal was clearly not enough.

"Do it for your mother, at the very least," her father added in a tone laced with intimidation. She knew her father well enough. He'd humiliate his wife even more if their daughter didn't cooperate.

"You know I'd do anything for her."

He smiled at her with something close to warmth. "You're a smart girl, I'll give you that." His gaze brushed over her plain abaya. "And pleasant enough to look at, even with your western appearance."

"Does it bother you that I look like my mother and not you?"

His jaw tightened fractionally. "Looks fade, Yasmine. Your mother is proof of that."

Yasmine was so stunned by his insult she didn't even have the ability to counter one better. Her mother was still a gorgeous woman, despite her forty-five years. Her fifty-nine year old father was blessed to have her.

A guard was already standing at Yasmine's bedroom suite door, and her father took hold of her arm as the guard opened the door. "Don't do anything to stuff this up, Yasmine. Too many are depending on this marriage now."

She managed a smile. "Oh, I won't. I'm all too aware I dodged a bullet." She stepped inside, then turned around to his frowning, and perhaps guilty countenance, and added, "Please give my regards to the old goat, Arif. I'm sure he can't wait to hear about the change of plans."

# Chapter Five

Yasmine snuck a peak at her new husband, Sheikh Jamal, made suddenly breathless by the power he emanated, her nerves fluttering with anticipation. He'd clasped her hand, the one with the priceless engagement ring and now its matching wedding ring on her finger, and led her down one of the many wide corridors of his palace toward his bedroom suite.

The palace corridors and the few rooms she'd peeked into that had been open were impeccable, with not even a dust mote daring to hang in the air. That was despite the fact somewhere in the palace some kind of construction was going on, with the grinding and hammering of building tools reaching her ears.

"I've commissioned someone to build a ballroom," he explained with a wry smile.

"Really?" So he could dance as well as run a country and keep its people wealthy and happy? It seemed unfair for one man to have so many talents. "I can't wait to see it."

He chuckled. "And I'm looking forward to sweeping you around on its floor."

That it'd happen sooner rather than later wasn't lost on her. It seemed impossible to believe what had already transpired in such a short time. It'd been three days since her father had caught her in bed with Jamal. Two days later Jamal had presented her with an exquisite diamond engagement ring before they'd made their official announcement in her homeland of Amack, where a whirlwind of celebrations was condensed into one day.

This morning she and Jamal, along with her family and friends, had flown to Jamal's country, where she'd exchanged vows with him.

She was now the Sheikha of Ishmat. And though she was exhausted and a little bit frightened, she was also exhilarated at what lay ahead. Her future was a whole lot brighter now she was no longer suffocated by bleak thoughts of marrying a despot.

That she hid another, entirely different secret, one that involved sneaking a daily birth control pill, was yet another deception she'd gladly learn to live with. She'd have children when she was ready and not beforehand. She was only lucky her doctor was forward thinking and hadn't felt the need to confer with Jamal.

*My body. My choice.*

"This way," Jamal murmured, drawing her past an open room that featured mosaic tiles, a lap pool with water cascading at one end, and seating areas half-hidden by big urns with lacy green plants.

He swung open a door then bent and lifted her against his chest. "Allow me to carry my wife across the threshold."

She giggled even as she noted the flex and shift of his muscles, the effortless way he carried her. There really was something compelling about his strength. He didn't get this strong by being idle and getting everyone else to do his work for him. Add in his scent of sandalwood and warm cinnamon and she was all but drooling.

He kicked the door shut behind him and she blinked up at his suddenly serious face. "No regrets?"

He gazed down at her, his long lashes half-concealing his thoughts. "I don't make it habit to have regrets. Once my mind is made up nothing can make me change it." He thumbed a piece of her blonde hair back under her delicate, flower-embroidered hijab with attached veil. "I'll do whatever it takes to make you happy."

She swallowed hard at his words, torn between joyous relief and a shiver of premonition she couldn't quite shake off. She ignored it anyway and said softly, "And I'll do everything I can to make you happy in return."

It was an indelible moment. They might not love one another—they were barely more than strangers—but he'd taken his vows as seriously as she had and his latest words confirmed that.

That she was wildly attracted to him was just the icing on the cake. From his designer facial stubble and styled dark hair, his brilliant dark eyes that appeared to decipher absolutely everything, to his broad shoulders and narrow waist, his strong thighs and impressive cock, he was her perfect husband.

The moment he bent and captured her mouth with his own, she was lost to him. Winding her arms behind his neck, she kissed him in return, her body past ready for him to take her all the way and show her exactly how good sex should be.

He drew back and his eyes glinted down at her. "Not so fast, angel. You were a virgin our first time together. I want to slow it down and make sure you're ready for me this time."

"Ready for you?" she repeated weakly.

His smile broadened. "You really are an innocent aren't you? It must have taken everything you had to deceive me into thinking you were a harem girl."

Guilt hollowed out her stomach. But he didn't look angry. Perhaps he was good at hiding his emotions and had something vengeful planned for her?

"No need to look so anxious," he added with a faint frown. "I'll take good care of you."

She managed to push back uncertainty as he lifted his hands to take off her hijab, unpinning her hair then with meticulous care. He groaned as her blonde tresses spilled free, his jaw tight as he then unbuttoned the back of her gauzy wedding dress with its diamond inserts.

The gown slipped free and he drank in her bared body covered in nothing more than tiny slips of silk, cream underwear. "So beautiful," he said reverently.

She stood uncertainly as he unbuttoned his tailored suit jacket, then started on his white dress shirt.

"Allow me," she said with a little tremor in her voice.

He nodded and she undid the last three buttons of his shirt, exposing the golden skin of his torso, the ridged muscles of his flat stomach. She swallowed as she pushed his jacket over his shoulders, followed by his shirt.

She'd like to pretend she'd forgotten about his sheer masculine perfection, but she'd be lying. She'd memorized every part of him, even the light dusting of hair that started from his navel and disappeared beneath the waistband of his black pants.

She looked down to undo his pants, the distinct bulge of his groin flooding her with warmth while quiet terror left her quaking inside.

His breath hissed as her fingertips scraped the bared skin above his pants. A hiss that grew harder—along with his cock—when she tentatively brushed his bulging erection.

"You're killing me," he said hoarsely.

Her nerves jumped and she dropped her arms back to her sides. "Am I doing something wrong?"

He exhaled slowly. "No. You're doing everything right." He reached for her. "Come here."

She stepped closer and he brushed his big, capable hands over her shoulders and down her back, stopping at her bra clasp. "Allow me," he said, then unfastened her bra to free her breasts.

Despite the fact he'd seen her nude once before, sudden shyness overwhelmed her and it took everything she had not to cover herself with her hands. She mightn't be small but she certainly wasn't bountiful in the breast department. Yet the moment his eyes lit up with appreciation all her reserve melted away.

"Exquisite," he breathed.

It gave her the confidence needed to reach for the button and zipper on his pants once again. This time she managed to undo them before she pulled his pants over his hips and past his knees. Though he wore snug boxer briefs, the close-up, tantalizing view of his erection left her too weak to do anything but stare.

Jamal chuckled and clasped her hands to draw her back upright. "I'll be more careful this time, I promise." His breath touched her ear, sending goosebumps to her core even before he added, "Soon enough your body will accept mine. We were made for one another."

His reassurance heightened her awareness of him. Reminded her how big, powerful and experienced he was compared to her far smaller stature and naïve innocence.

He toed off his shoes and stepped out of his pants, and they faced one another in nothing but their underpants. It took every ounce of her courage to hook her thumbs into her little silk panties and draw them down, exposing her entire body to his heated gaze.

A pulse jerked into life at one side of his jaw as he followed suit and drew off his boxer briefs, his cock springing free, impressively big and hard.

It wasn't until a whimper of something between need and denial built in her throat and escaped, that he cupped her face and bent to kiss her once again. His soft lips pillowed hers while his unyielding mouth grew even more demanding, his cock twitching against her belly.

When he eventually released her, he was breathing heavily, his face flushed and his dick harder than a concrete pillar. But instead of taking her and easing his lust, he took her hand and said, "Come."

She stifled sudden hysteria. He'd barely touched her and she was already close to coming. If this was the foreplay he'd promised before they had sex again then she wasn't complaining.

It wasn't until he stepped into the shower and turned on the double showerheads that she realized this was just the beginning of preparing her body for his possession. She gulped as he drew her around so that her back was against his front. Pouring some liquid body wash into his palm, he rubbed his hands to create bubbles, then massaged them all over her front while paying particular attention to her breasts.

It didn't take long for her anxiety to fade and her body to loosen. She was little more than a blissful lump of putty as he caressed her ever hardening nipples, then swept the bubbles over her shoulders, her collarbone, her ribs...everywhere. A flame burned through her veins to center at her core, until she was burning up for him and ready for more.

He slid a hand between her legs and she jerked with a gasp as he began kneading her clitoris. Pleasure flooded through her and her bud swelled at his touch, begging for more. With his cock pressing insistently against her back, she pushed up onto her tiptoes, desperate to feel him between her thighs.

His chuckle reverberated through her, heightening her lust until she couldn't resist gyrating against him. She felt his tension, literally, but he had to have steely willpower when he continued soaping her all over, focused now on her back and buttocks, all the way down her legs, before he rinsed her and turned off the pressure. "Let's get you dry."

It was strangely erotic allowing him to rub her with a big, soft white towel, where he was particularly devoted to her breasts, and then between her legs, dragging the towel back and forth while her pleasure built and built.

She groaned hoarsely when he threw the towel into a chute and it disappeared from sight to a laundry room. But if she thought she'd succumbed completely to him then he was in for a rude shock.

"Allow me," she said huskily.

She pulled free another towel from its heated rack, and wound it around his neck to drag it slowly back and forth. Moving it down his back an inch at a time until she was crouched at eye-level to his cock and she was drying the water off the back of his thighs.

She started on his front then, his ankles first, his shins, his thighs and finally his cock that strained toward her like a heat-seeking missile.

She *was* hot, combusting with passion and need.

She kissed his cock head, wanting onto to taste him, to feel the satin-smooth skin overlaying pulsating hardness.

He groaned, and drew her back up, his dark eyes savage with their intensity. "I don't know what it is about you but it's taking everything I have not to have you here and now, and without any restraint."

She blinked up at him, no longer feeling inferior or intimidated by her lack of height. She'd never felt more powerful, a tigress who'd unleashed her claws for the first time. "What's stopping you?" she asked huskily.

He exhaled and bent to pick her up. Only when she was pressed against his chest, his heartbeat thundering close to her ears, did he respond, "You're still an innocent and I'm not an unfeeling jerk." He carried her back into his bedroom and laid her onto the mattress. "Not yet anyway. You'll see my uncivilized side soon enough."

She didn't have the ability to think let alone ask what exactly he meant by that when kissed his way down her torso, his head then stilling between her thighs as he parted the outer folds of her pussy. She stiffened somewhere between shock and anticipation before his first lick sent her gasping and breathless. His second, third and fourth burned through her bundle of nerves with ever-powerful jolts of electricity.

She was no longer self-conscious in any way, with her thighs spread open in invitation, her indistinct moans becoming louder and sharper as an orgasm beckoned.

Then he sucked hard on her plump bud and she shattered with a cry of ecstasy, one that grew in volume when he didn't relent, his tongue flicking like a whip and leaving her wrung out with pleasure and unable to utter a single coherent word.

He smiled when he finally climbed back over her and took her mouth with his, ensuring she tasted herself on his lips and his tongue before he lifted his head and said hoarsely, "You're ready for me now. You belong to me."

# Chapter Six

Jamal had never been so close to prematurely spilling his seed and disgracing himself. What was it about his wife that sent him so close to the edge? Maybe it was because he hadn't stopped thinking about her from the moment he'd seen her. That entering her body without finishing what he'd started had almost sent him mad with lust was just an added complication.

Not half as complicated as being tricked into marrying her, a little voice in his head reminded.

The voice of reason didn't stop him aligning his shaft to her inviting wetness. He adored problem solving almost as much as he adored his gorgeous wife.

From her golden skin and her silver-blonde hair, her cornflower blue eyes and luscious pink lips, her small but perfectly formed breasts and her pussy that had made his mouth water for just one taste, she was his perfect match in every way. That she was smart—he'd recently learned she had a business and modern languages degree—only added fuel to his flames of desire.

She was perfection in every way.

Then he plunged inside her and all thought ceased to exist, only pleasure. She was as tight as their first time, her inner muscles locking around him and her gasp of pain reminding him that he was bigger than most men. That he had to restrain his beast mode and take it slow and gentle half-killed him.

Until the moment she softened beneath him, her gasps becoming as slumberous as her beautiful eyes. He pushed in and out, her breasts jiggling while her moisture lubed his shaft and made him slick.

Her gasps soon became moans and she was writhing beneath him while he stroked inside her harder and faster, and he was somewhere between heaven and hell as he forced himself not to come. Not yet. Not until her eyes popped wide open and she mewled like a cat as she climaxed, her inner muscles grasping and grabbing.

He plunged deep, releasing his seed with a roar, his pleasure so intense his eyes rolled and he saw everything through a red haze of lust. *Fuck.* He'd never experienced anything near as sublime as this release.

That he was left dazed and disoriented spoke volumes about his many other sexual encounters. He'd been left satisfied yet empty.

With Yasmine he was fulfilled in every way that counted. It was so unexpected he didn't know what to think...what to feel.

"Are you okay?" she asked softly.

He resisted shaking his head to clear it. He didn't want her to misinterpret that as a *no*. "I should be asking you that."

She smiled, a shaky, tremulous smile that tore at his heartstrings. "At least now I understand why so many women want to join a harem."

Thanks to her dad, he had a feeling she knew firsthand that being in a harem wasn't just about sex and pleasure. "There is a rivalry in a harem like none other, the competition for attention fierce."

She nodded, then bit into her bottom lip as she looked up at him. "You sound very...knowledgeable. Do you have a harem?"

"Would it worry you if I did?" he asked gently.

Her lashes fluttered and she jostled a little beneath him, as though ready to abandon him and his personal questions. But he was in no mood to disconnect from her now. There was something right in staying bonded with her, their breaths in synch and his forearms taking most his weight while he looked down at her and read her like an open book.

"It worried my mother. She might be my dad's only wife but she has many beautiful harem women to contend with." She sighed. "She was raised in a western world, where most marriages signify loyalty and faithfulness to one another."

Right now he couldn't agree more with the western cultural belief. He didn't want anyone else but his silver-haired wife. She was his one and only. His bachelor past only confirmed his newfound belief. He'd been with enough women to know none of them interested him now he had Yasmine as his wife.

She blinked up at him. "I think those ingrained beliefs drove her half-mad with envy and injustice."

He brushed some hair off his wife's flushed face, his heart jerking erratically that he had the rest of his life to worship this gorgeous woman. "You were educated for a few years in London, too?"

"Yes." Her eyes widened. "How did you know?"

He winked. "I was compelled to research everything about my future wife."

Her eyes sparkled and her lush lips tilted up at the corners. "I hope I didn't disappoint you?"

"Hardly." He leaned down to capture her lips with his once again, enjoying her response that was as artless as it was passionate. Even her light freesia and vanilla scent captivated him.

He was going to enjoy every minute with his wife.

She sighed softly, then admitted, "I researched you, too."

"You did?" But of course she did. She wouldn't have set-up just anyone to sleep with and then force into marriage.

She nodded. "You have a good heart. You're smart and fair. And your people love you."

A glow started somewhere inside his chest and it took everything he had not to simply open himself up to her and give her the ability to rip out his heart. "I'm fair," he conceded, "but I can be unforgiving when warranted."

"And that is what makes you a great leader."

He arched a brow. "You are good at stroking a man's ego."

She giggled. "As good as I was at stroking your cock?"

He chuckled, though his shaft thickened and throbbed. "You're a natural at both."

She wound her arms around his neck. "I think I'm going to like being your wife, Sheikh Jamal."

His inner glow spread and infused every cell of his body. That it was as wonderful as it was unsettling wasn't something he wanted to think too deeply about. He was by nature a cautious man and he knew to trust his instincts.

This woman had the power to hurt him deeply.

That he was willing to take that chance showed just how serious he was about her. He needed her in his life.

His dick was rock-hard when he kissed her again and murmured, "Let's make that family we so desperately want."

She stiffened beneath him and Jamal frowned. "Is something wrong?"

She held his gaze, but her eyes were no longer open, they were shadowed and filled with secrets when she asked, "Will you have sex with your harem women while you're married to me?"

Why did he get the feeling she was evading his question by asking another one?

He shook his head. "It's just you and me, angel. I don't and have never had a harem."

Her stare widened. "Really?"

He smiled down at her. "Don't sound so surprised. I'm wealthy and powerful enough to have women throwing themselves at me without needing a harem on the side. And you said it yourself, I'm a fair man. I don't expect you to put up with me being with other women when I expect you all to myself in return."

"If only my dad thought the same way about my mother," she said softly.

How much had Yasmine's relationship with her dad affected her trust with other men? He only hoped she'd learn to trust him. He stroked slowly inside her and like a flower her body opened up for him, blossomed.

Soon enough he hoped her mind would do the same.

# Chapter Seven

"Rise and shine angel!"

Jamal's voice penetrated Yasmine's subconscious and she blinked as he opened the bedroom blinds and sunlight poured through the window and over his partially naked body.

Dear Lord, the towel wrapped low on his hips should be illegal.

"I can take it off if you prefer," he purred.

*Shit.* She'd said that out loud?

Her face heated. "I already know what's underneath."

He chuckled. "I'm just glad you appreciate it."

It *was* rather hard not to appreciate his assets. She stretched and yawned. "Please tell me it's midday already. I'm not getting up for anything other than lunch."

"Not even for what's underneath my towel?" he asked with a grin. At her tragic moan, he added, "Guess you're not a morning person. Good to know."

A knock sounded at the door and her husband called out, "Come in." A middle-aged woman in a gray headscarf and black hijab entered and he said brusquely, "Ah good, Farrah. Pack us each a suitcase of clothes, enough to last the week."

Yasmine sat up. "We're going away for a week?"

Jamal nodded and winked. "Of course. We're not spending our honeymoon here." He turned back to the servant. "A few pieces of swimwear, one or two evening outfits, some underwear and sleepwear. Oh, and some walking shoes." He chuckled. "We'll do some exploring...at some stage, I guess."

Yasmine's face grew warm, but Farrah was immune to any marital connotations, just as she seemed to somehow be immune to Jamal's half-naked body. She was already busy retrieving two pieces of leather luggage and filling it with the required clothing.

It was only once Yasmine went to get up that she remembered she was completely nude. Jamal's eyes glinted with repressed laughter as she once again wrapped a blanket around her body.

"Relax Yasmine. As my wife you're expected to be naked."

"Then I guess I should get used to it." She dropped the blanket and sashayed toward the bathroom, her husband's dark laughter following her.

She turned on the double showerheads and stepped under the spray, her whole body warm. Marriage was so much better than she'd ever imagined. But then her husband was so much better than she'd ever imagined, too.

Her gamble to trick him into being with her had paid off big time. Not only did Jamal treat her well, he took care of her needs in bed. Her stomach clenched. That might change when she failed to fall pregnant and he discovered she'd deceived him yet again.

"I'm so tempted to join you."

She started and spun around guiltily, as though her watchful husband could read her thoughts. She managed to smile brightly and again resisted covering her nakedness. "What time did you say you wanted to leave?"

"I didn't." He smirked a little. "But point taken. Once you're dressed we'll leave. We'll have brunch once we get there."

She arched a brow. "It can't be much past 9 a.m.?" Jamal's palace was on the outskirts of Ishmat's capital city, Al-Maya, so it made sense they didn't have to travel far for their honeymoon. "I'm guessing wherever we're going it must be by car."

"That's right." His eyes darkened as she turned off the taps and stepped out of the shower, then dried herself. "I like that my wife is beautiful and smart."

She straightened, aware of his eyes lingering on her pussy and then her breasts. Heightened self-awareness zinged through her. "And I like that you appreciate my body as much as I appreciate yours."

Though she was tempted to show off her body a little longer, she cleared her throat to drag back his attention. "I'm glad you have no problem with a wife who knows how to use her brain."

She wrapped the towel around her and he smiled as he lifted her chin with a hand and kissed her gently. He pulled back and his eyes held hers when he said, "You will be the mother of our children. I hope and expect they'll be as smart and beautiful as you."

That she had no intention of giving him what he wanted made her insides twist with guilt. "Or they might take after you," she answered, hiding her empty, stricken voice with an attempt at humor.

He chuckled, taking no offense. "There's always that risk," he conceded with a warm glint in his eyes. "We should probably get dressed," he added.

# Chapter Eight

Jamal had always enjoyed driving his own vehicles, but he still had to allow for some concessions. Such as the bullet proof glass and reinforced metal that made up the body of the jeep he'd chosen.

There was also his security detail, his trained combat men who drove in front and behind his vehicle. The men were essential, particularly in the city where endless alleyways, buildings and hideaways made such an attack more likely. Though he was loved by his people there were always enemies waiting to take him down, enemies that now included Sheikh Arif.

At least once Jamal and his wife were inside the safety of his most recently built resort, his security could fade back and become much more discreet, leaving him and Yasmine mostly to their own devices.

He glanced at his wife, his heart thudding a little harder as all his protective instincts rose up inside him. She looked gorgeous in her white sundress and pretty little heeled sandals.

She really was his angel.

How had her father even considered giving her away to the fat, cruel Arif? The man might be wealthy but he wasn't honorable and didn't have a kind bone in his body. Yasmine would have become a shell of her now beautiful, glorious self.

His scalp prickled and his stomach hardened. He might actually need to increase security until he got word on how Arif had reacted to Yasmine marrying someone else. That she'd married a younger, wealthier and more powerful sheikh would undoubtedly have rubbed salt into Arif's already wounded dignity and pride.

*Too bad.* The old sheikh didn't deserve her. He didn't deserve any woman.

Yasmine's face was even now open with delight as she gazed at the modern city with its sculptures and steel and glass structures mixed with ancient buildings and artifacts. Spice markets cropped up here and there amongst it all so that even inside the air-conditioned jeep the scent of cinnamon and ginger permeated, and most notably, the floral yet metallic notes of saffron.

"You are captivated by everything you see. Were you not allowed to explore outside your father's palace?" he asked, just barely withholding a growl at the thought of her locked away like some well-guarded investment.

She grimaced. "Dad was very protective of me. I only wish it was because he cared about me like a father should. Instead he was more worried about the taint of my western blood affecting my decision making with men."

"Then he's a fool." Jamal wanted nothing more than to force Zameer into acknowledging the beautiful daughter he'd been lucky to have. It was rumored the old sheikh was infertile, so any child was a blessing.

Jamal's hands tightened on the steering wheel, his senses prickling. Was there more to his wife's background than what he'd even considered? He made a mental note to get in contact with a PI whose success rate was legendary. Of course the man was exorbitantly priced and therefore unavailable to anyone but the super-rich, but Jamal had no problem with that.

It wouldn't even put a dent his bank account to have his wife investigated and erase any doubt about her pedigree. His lips twitched. Not that it bothered him if her bloodline wasn't what he'd imagined. She was his perfect match.

Her usually light, tinkling laugh sounded raw. "Except I've proven him right now after he caught me in bed with you." She sighed softly.

"It must have taken every bit of my mom's arsenal to convince him to allow me to travel to the UK and study for a couple of years to broaden my horizons."

Jamal didn't want to think about what sacrifices her mother had been forced to endure with Zameer to let their daughter go. The western culture was mostly frowned upon by the people of his world, especially when it came to their women. And though Zameer was modern enough to share a select number of his harem with esteemed guests, Yasmine would be regarded as an asset, an innocent pawn in the game of advancement.

She might feel cheapened by her father's behavior, but in truth her unique, western looks were priceless to Zameer.

Jamal shuddered to think of what would have happened to Yasmine if she hadn't decided to ensnare him in bed before her arranged marriage to Sheikh Arif had been enforced.

"Oh, look," she said, pointing at a string of camels walking sedately in a line with wares tied to their backs, a lone man leading them alongside the road. "I've always wanted to ride a camel."

"Really?"

She nodded. "My dad isn't into camels, he breeds Arabian racehorses."

Jamal was aware of her father's horses. But for those buyers wanting a champion racehorse, they simply couldn't go past Fayez's quality horses, which all too often outraced Zameer's.

Her dad hadn't just been set in his ways about their failing tourism. He also still stubbornly backed his own racehorses.

Jamal pushed aside his thoughts and raised a brow. "Riding a camel is nothing short of torture," he said with a grim smile.

He should know. He and his friends, Mahindar and Fayez, had agreed to a dare made by their other close friend, Hamid. They'd lost the bet, which had then seen them having to race camels in the nude in the baking hot, desert heat. They'd all been sunburned, bruised and sore for a week after. Not to mention just a little bit humiliated.

Yet the memory was a fond one that he and his friends often discussed and laughed about, their friendship with Hamid still as strong as ever. Especially now their betting friend had lost his biggest gamble of all by falling in love.

That Hamid loved his wife even more than his drinking and gambling, his camels and the desert, still shocked Jamal. He'd never thought he'd see the day Hamid would choose a woman over any one of those things. Yet Hamid was now happily married and living his best life.

Jamal glanced at Yasmine once again. It was only now that he was married himself and already developing strong feelings for his wife that he understood Hamid's change of heart. Jamal would sacrifice anything to keep Yasmine happy, just as he'd do anything to make her fall in love with him.

It was a heady and exhilarating epiphany, but it was also one that shook him to the core. What if she never fell in love? What if she was happy just to escape a future that would have been full of sick depravity and humiliation if she'd been forced to instead wed Arif?

Jamal had never wanted commitment from anyone before, quite the opposite. Those women who'd believed he was the love of their lives had left him cold and with no desire for a long-term relationship. Give him one night stands any day of the week, a physical release without any emotion entanglements.

How things had changed.

Perhaps Karma had interceded to teach him a lesson? He'd been a confirmed bachelor with absolutely no desire to change his ways. Then he'd taken one look at Yasmine, and actually cared about her predicament, and he'd been lost to her. And willing to do whatever was needed to keep her safe and by his side.

He was yet to discover if he'd become the world's biggest fool, or the smartest man on the planet.

# Chapter Nine

Yasmine's pulse picked up speed as Jamal turned into a driveway. It cut between high, impenetrable walls of sandstone, where the tops of date palms poked over the wall and rustled in a salt-laden breeze, the greenery softening an otherwise austere look.

The first security car slowed then stopped at the fancy black, wrought iron gates, which immediately opened for them. She read the gold lettering in the center of the gates. *Qadir Palms Resort.*

She blinked, then turned to him. "You built this resort?"

He grinned. "This one was a bit of a pet project. I had dredged sand brought in to make up most of the land the resort sits on."

*Holy crap.* The resort would have cost him millions. Perhaps billions. Little wonder her father had been pleased she'd trapped Jamal into marriage. That her dear old dad expected her to extract even more money to continue helping to save her homeland from financial ruin made her stomach clench.

She wasn't a gold digger, but that was what her dad was making her. Jamal's dowry had no doubt only whetted her dad's appetite for more.

Jamal followed the lead car past the security gates and down a smooth, tree-lined road, the ocean a sparkling azure blanket either side of them. Super yachts and speed boats were moored safely in the manmade harbor, revealing the exclusivity of the resort. A trio of men had fun riding big shiny jet skis on the water, with salty trails of white left in their wake.

The land widened and the road split left and right, a glorious garden in the center showcasing lacy plants and tall spiked flowers. On one side three tall, curved buildings with balconies revealed holiday apartments. To the right, the road Jamal and his security detail took, little villas with thatched roofs sat over the ocean, each one showcasing a deck with their own infinity pool.

Jamal smiled at her and reached over to clasp her hand. "We call these the honeymoon huts," he said, then lifted her hand to kiss her knuckles. "I thought you might prefer being close to the ocean."

She gaped. "They're perfect!"

As a sheikha she'd lived a relatively isolated life and had never really been anywhere besides her father's palace and heavily guarded trips to the city and the markets. She'd had more freedom in England where she'd attended university, and had regularly enjoyed lunch and dinner outings at a nearby coffee shop and bar, but mostly she'd kept her head down and studied hard.

Doing anything more risqué would have seen her opportunity to study overseas forfeited.

As it was her father had sent at least two bodyguards to keep an eye on her. When she'd gotten too close to one of them he'd left university without even a goodbye, vanishing as though he'd never been. She'd enjoyed his company while it'd lasted. But although he'd seemed normal enough, his easy smile and charm had overlaid an intrinsic caution that had aroused her suspicions of his true identity.

His so called best friend had been the same way, his eyes watchful and distrustful, as though awaiting attack. The only difference was that he'd stayed distant to her and therefore hadn't needed to leave his "studies."

Jamal nodded with a satisfied smile. "The huts are self-sufficient and come with a fully stocked fridge and pantry. And no television or internet. Just swimming, snorkeling, relaxing," he chuckled, "and sex. These villas were designed for honeymooners without the outside world encroaching on them."

"It sounds wonderful."

Though her husband overwhelmed her with his experience and power, she was up for the challenge. She wanted to be his equal in every way. Well...perhaps not *every* way. She enjoyed his dominance even as she sensed he'd held back thanks to her inexperience.

Not for much longer. She wasn't made of glass. She wanted to be claimed by him without reserve. She wanted to enjoy the full force of his possession.

His gaze glinted as he glanced at her, a possessive touch to his eyes. "What better way to fully get to know one another?"

She couldn't argue there. Excitement and anticipation pulsed through her and she couldn't help but clap her hands when he pulled in front of what must be their hut. Except this one was completely secluded, with potted greenery and a screen enclosing the deck and giving them added privacy from the nearest hut.

The other side of their hut had no one to encroach on their views or their isolation. What was left of the sand spit narrowed dramatically before giving away to the sea.

Not even the taller apartment buildings that sat farther back encroached on their privacy.

She didn't wait for her husband to open her door. She clambered out of the car and put a hand over her eyes to shield against the bright, midmorning sun, taking in what was to be their dwelling for the next seven days. She shivered. This was just the start of her life changing journey.

"Are you okay?" Jamal asked, his stare all too perceptive as he came to stand beside her.

Damn he was big, she was lucky to reach his shoulder. That he was dressed in western pants and a white shirt only made him seem more impressively powerful.

She brushed at her goose-bumped arms. "I guess I'm just a little overwhelmed."

"You married a stranger. You wouldn't be human if you weren't a little bit dazed by it all."

"You're probably right." She bit her bottom lip. "How are you feeling about us?"

He grinned. "No regrets, remember. I know what I want, angel. And what I want is you."

Another shiver slipped down her spine. Being wanted was flattering and scary all at once. He did seem into her. But what if he lost interest? What if his feelings died and he wished he'd never agreed to marry her?

*Ugh.* She had to stop looking for holes in their marriage and enjoy his interest and attention while it lasted. Nothing was forever but maybe, just maybe, their wedded bliss wouldn't completely fade.

She dragged her gaze away from the intensity of his stare to again focus on their honeymoon villa. Its bamboo walls and thatched roof gave it a Bali vibe and she itched to see the inside. She'd bet it was the premium hut. Not only did it sit farther out on the ocean, where a boardwalk gave them access, but going by the size of the deck it also had a far bigger infinity pool.

She stepped toward the boardwalk and Jamal reached out to stop her. "Not yet." He nodded toward the security men, whose vehicles still flanked their jeep front and back. The drivers alighted and one walked across the boardwalk and inside the hut to check for possible intruders while the other grabbed her and Jamal's luggage from out of the jeep.

The security guy who'd entered the hut stepped out a minute later, and nodded deferentially at Jamal. "All clear."

Jamal turned back to her, and swept out his hand. "After you."

She managed a smile, but the euphoria of earlier had diminished, all her self-doubts returning with a vengeance. Was she as trapped living with her husband as she'd been living with her father?

*At least Jamal makes you happy.*

"Your mood's changed," he observed as they stepped onto the boardwalk and then inside the hut, their security men bringing their luggage from behind.

She bit her bottom lip. "I just wish things weren't so complicated."

"Like having security with us and being overly cautious?"

She nodded. "I'd do anything to have a normal life."

He exhaled slowly. "And yet you're a sheikha now married to a sheikh. Normal doesn't come with the territory."

She sighed. "No, it really doesn't."

Despite her sudden melancholy, it didn't take long for Jamal to cheer her up. Once his security detail had faded away, possibly to one of the other huts, he pointed out the dark-stained, exposed timber beams, the airy kitchen that was surprisingly modern and spacious, the plush bedroom with its king bed and fresh seashell print cover, and the en suite with its welcome basket of goodies on the double vanity showcasing lotions, soaps, body wash, candles and more.

Then Jamal placed his big hands on her shoulders and turned her around to face him. "I need you," he stated simply.

A thrill shot through her. She loved how much her husband desired her. Though it might only be for sex it was a start, something she could build on. With a little influence, some divine intervention and a lot of luck, he'd soon want far more from her than sex alone.

For now though, it was enough.

She smiled up at him. It was *more* than enough.

# Chapter Ten

One day seemed to merge into the other until day five of their seven day honeymoon was upon them. It'd taken around three of those days for Yasmine to surrender completely to the happiness that consumed her, managing to push away any and all dark thoughts to focus wholly on her husband.

She wanted to delight him as much as he delighted her. The sex between them was incredible, their bond deepening quickly with each and every time they made love.

When they weren't exploring one another, they were exploring the sea together hand-in-hand while they snorkeled and swam, colorful fish darting around them and turtles occasionally making an appearance.

Yasmine enjoyed their seclusion so much she'd even taken to swimming naked in their infinity pool, then sunbathing under the sun's rays until her husband couldn't take the temptation anymore and he took her right where she lay.

She turned her head from where she was sprawled on her deck lounge, blinking at her husband lying next to her with his eyes shut and seemingly half-asleep. She grinned. He'd restrained himself admirably so far this morning, but as much as she was tempted to change his mind by testing out some of her newfound seduction techniques, her body was a little sore from all their physical intimacy.

Not that she was complaining. She'd wanted him unrestrained and he'd readily obliged. He'd pounded into her from behind, then against a wall, in the shower and over the kitchen counter. There was barely a surface inside and outside the villa they hadn't inducted into their sexual activities.

She no longer needed a bathroom mirror to be amazed by her glow of inner happiness and fulfilment. She'd never looked so good. Their honeymoon had been good for him, too. He was relaxed and at peace, the weight of his many responsibilities seemingly taken off his shoulders.

She reached out and traced a hand over his corded arm, his sun-kissed, golden skin flecking with goose bumps.

"Keep touching me like that and nothing will hold me back from you."

"Is that a threat or a promise?" she purred.

His eyelids flicked open, his dark gaze holding hers. "I promised you many children, angel. I won't stop having sex with you until your belly is rounded with our son or daughter."

She swallowed hard, her joy evaporating. "So the moment you succeed in getting me pregnant you'll leave me alone?"

He chuckled. "I could no more do that than a starving dog could leave alone a meaty bone. But I will be more careful. I won't risk our unborn child."

What would he say if he learned of her being on birth control?

Her throat dried. "You want children *that* badly?"

He blinked, and this once she wasn't intoxicated by his sheer masculine beauty, his body's powerful lines, and the long length of his cock that thickened even as they talked. She was too busy trying to read his fathomless dark gaze.

"It would be your greatest gift to me," he said simply.

*Shit.*

She pressed her hands to her churning stomach. "We mightn't have children for many years."

"Or we could have a great many children in a short time," he refuted gently. He sat, his shadow falling over her and blocking out much of the sun. "If you're afraid you mightn't conceive then let me reassure—"

"*No.* There's no need for that," she interjected quickly.

His gaze penetrated hers. "You *do* want to be a mother, don't you?"

Sweat beaded on her brow. "One day," she hedged. She couldn't tell him the truth, but she couldn't pretend innocence, either. Yasmine had seen how badly it had affected her mother when her dad had gone to other women after being unable to give him the son he'd wanted.

Her breath punched out while a dozen questions filled her head. Had she inherited that same trait? *Was* she infertile, too? Was she needlessly on birth control?

She cleared her throat. "What's with the serious conversation?"

He arched a dark brow. "You'd rather we discuss the weather?"

*Yes, actually.*

His eyes narrowed speculatively at her silence. "We're married, angel. Discussing our future family shouldn't be so hard."

She swiped a hand through her hair, her breasts jiggling at the motion and immediately distracting him. Who needed words when she had a pair of breasts in her arsenal? She pushed her chest out and fluttered her lashes. "Well it's stifling out here and I'm ready for a dip. Care to join me?"

He pushed to his feet, then proffered his hand to pull her up. "A swim. Then we talk."

Her throat dry, she walked across the deck that was hot underfoot. Jamal wouldn't be put off again. Not even sex would distract him next time. That his latent power and size left her shivering between desire and fear caused her to snatch her hand free and dive into the cool water, bubbles fizzing past her face.

*Plunk.*

She looked back as he dived in, following her like a torpedo through the water. Her breath expelled in a burst of bubbles as he swept her into his arms and kicked upward until their heads popped above the water. His eyes dark with passion, he slammed his mouth onto hers, stealing her breath all over again.

She sucked the air out of his lungs and kissed him right back, and he groaned low and deep as he waded to the shallow end. Jerking his mouth from hers, he turned her around and leaned her over the edge of the pool. Then nuzzling her throat from behind, he said hoarsely, "I don't know that I'll ever get enough of you."

"Ditto," she gasped.

He caressed her butt and then her inner thigh with one hand, before parting her folds to thumb her clit with the other. She groaned in response and pushed against him, the ache inside now unbearable.

He rotated her fleshy bundle of nerves harder and faster, and she whimpered at the overwhelming pleasure that built quickly within. She was still unprepared for the explosive orgasm that flashed through her like an electric shock and left her insides wrenching with aftershocks.

"Your body is made for mine, angel."

She was still climaxing when he thrust inside her, and he exhaled harshly as her inner muscles clutched at his shaft. The pleasure-pain of his swollen cock buried deep inside almost sent her over the edge again. But if she was on the precipice then he was hanging on by his fingernails.

His strokes weren't refined. He pumped furiously inside her. Water sloshed rhythmically while her body accepted his with slick, wet heat and she once again succumbed to his mastery. She cried out his name as an even bigger climax sent her flying and she shattered in a kaleidoscope of pieces, then floated back to Earth in utter bliss.

Her pleasure seemed to stoke his, and he lasted perhaps a dozen more strokes before he too yielded to the moment with a stark growl, his whole body shuddering as he flooded her with his seed.

He slumped over her for long minutes, and there was something so satisfying in having him stay connected, his big body covering hers and his warm breath tickling her ear.

He kissed the back of her neck. "I need to slow things down."

"I'm not a virgin anymore," she mumbled, so relaxed and content she might just go to sleep right there on the sun-warmed deck.

"No, but I've been hammering your body when I should be taking it easy on you."

He drew back and pulled away from her before turning her to face him in the shallow water. Her legs trembled with the effort of standing after such delightful sex therapy, and she glared a little as she looked up at him.

"I was happy to never move again."

He smiled. "But then you wouldn't have time to get ready for our date tonight."

# Chapter Eleven

Yasmine turned off the shower and stepped out to dry herself. Pulling on a bathrobe, she got busy drying her hair with the hairdryer. She'd already picked out a light blue dress that would showcase her tan. She'd wear it with her hair upswept while leaving some tendrils free.

She was finishing putting her hair up into a twisted chignon when movement caught her eye. Her husband appeared behind her, his eyes gleaming. "I have a present for you."

She slid the last clip into her hair. "You do?"

He bent and kissed her bared nape. "Mmhm." Then lifting his hands he presented her with a stunning diamond choker that featured a pendent in the shape of a star. It glittered under the bathroom lights, enchanting her, and she stood wordlessly as he slipped it on and clasped it behind her neck.

"I love it," she breathed. "It will look perfect with my dress."

"It comes with matching stud earrings," he said with a pleased smile. "Once you're dressed you can put them on too."

Ten minutes later she slid in her earrings and stepped back to look at her reflection in the mirror. *Perfect.* The jewelry really was a stunning foil for her dress and upswept hair. Her husband had outstanding if expensive taste.

Jamal returned to the bathroom and stood behind her once again, his gaze admiring. "How did I get so lucky?"

"I should be the one saying that," she said, staring past the reflection of her glittery jewelry to the man who'd bought them for her. Even in her heels he towered over her, yet he made her feel safe, cherished.

"Well here's a little incentive." He pressed a gold-plated credit card into her hand. "I want you to have every advantage of being my wife. The funds are for you, buy whatever you want or need."

She stared at the card like it was a snake. "I don't need your money."

He smirked. "Said no woman ever." He kissed her nape. "Take it, angel. Enjoy it. Spend up big. The funds are unlimited. It will give me pleasure seeing your pleasure."

What was it about the card that made her insides twist with dread? Any other woman would be throwing their arms around their husband and squealing with joy.

She managed to smile. "You see that every time you take me to bed."

He chuckled. "True. But pleasure comes in many forms."

She opened up her clutch purse and stuck the card inside. "Thank you. You spoil me too much. I really am lucky."

He didn't seem to notice how hollow her words sounded.

"Then let's hope that same luck holds out for us tonight." Before she had a chance to get him to expand on where they were going, he proffered his arm. "If you're ready, angel, we'll go."

*

It'd been wonderful having her husband all to herself, but it was almost as exciting to step inside a casino crowded with people, wealth fairly screaming from the building and its patrons. Slot machines tinkled and buzzed, and gamblers crowded around gaming tables with excited shouts and groans.

She glanced at Jamal. He wore a white suit and a black dress shirt, the color highlighting his tan as much as her clingy, light blue dress showcased hers. She touched her glittery choker. She'd never been huge on precious jewels but having his gift on her body made her feel on top of the world, like nothing could ever drag them apart.

They really were newlyweds. Happy and devoted to one another.

That she'd worried he'd want to take his revenge out on her seemed so silly now. He wasn't that type of guy. He'd really meant it when he said he never regretted a decision once he'd made one.

She only hoped his one future regret wasn't that he'd married her.

Some loud cheers drew her gaze to the craps table, and Jamal smiled as he steered her toward the green velvet table where play was in full swing. "Want to try your luck at rolling the dice?" he asked.

"I'm not much of a gambler."

"That makes two of us," he conceded. "Hamid has always been the king when it comes to winning bets. But I still don't mind a flutter now and then, especially when any losses goes into my pocket eventually anyway."

She'd met Hamid and Jamal's other sheikh friends at their wedding. But though she'd noticed the other men's good looks and charisma she'd been too wrapped up in the man she was marrying. Nerves and adrenaline had prevented her from even thinking about anyone else.

She glanced at him. "Don't tell me you own this casino?"

He laughed. "Would it bother you if I did?"

She shook her head. "Not at all. I guess I'm more surprised at how many enterprises you have."

"I used to run myself ragged trying to oversee them all. Not anymore, though. I delegate the majority of my work to staff I trust. I'm as selective now with my time when it comes to business as I am to those I employ. What is the point of so much wealth if there isn't any time to relax and enjoy the fruits of my success?"

She swallowed as self-doubts roared into life. Was she one of the fruits of his success? An asset that he'd acquired?

He smiled down at her. "And now that I have a beautiful wife to keep me busy and on my toes I'll be delegating even more responsibility."

All her doubts dissolved at him wanting to spend more time with her, and she fairly beamed from the inside out as she smiled right back at him. "It's good to know I'll always have my husband's attention."

"You'll always be my priority, along with our future children."

Some of her joy dissipated. He was nothing short of obsessed with having children. There was only one way to divert his preoccupation of becoming a father. "If you do ever lose interest in me, I can think of a few possibilities in getting it back," she said huskily.

His delighted laugh seemed to fill the room, drawing the eyes of countless strangers. But if Jamal noticed he didn't let on, he simple put his arm around her waist and turned his attention to the craps table.

It was uncanny how fast the players made room for them, their demeanor far more respectful and subdued. But Yasmine didn't notice for long, she was too busy soaking in Jamal's brief rundown of rules while the man running the craps table—the stickman—turned over the off counter and passed her a bowl with five dice, asking her to select two of them.

"This is the come out roll," Jamal instructed, "and you're the new shooter." He gave her some big bills and she put them on the table, exchanging money for chips from the boxman. Jamal did the same, then placed a stack of chips on the pass line bet area on the table.

She threw the dice. After rolling seven from her two dice everyone cheered, with at least five people betting on her for the win.

Jamal pulled her close and kissed her. "Well done, angel. You really are my lucky charm."

She played at the craps table for another twenty minutes or so, winning more than losing her rounds, when one of their bodyguards approached and murmured something into Jamal's ear.

Jamal frowned and looked at Yasmine. "Your father is on the phone for you."

"He is?"

The bodyguard held up a cellphone, but it was far too noisy inside the casino. "I'll take this outside." When Jamal nodded and went to follow her she said, "No, please, stay here, enjoy your game. I'll be back soon enough. Your bodyguard won't let anything happen to me."

Jamal glanced at the man with the jagged white scar that dissected his beard on one side, and though a shiver of foreboding went down Yasmine's spine, she was intrigued too, and wondered if the bodyguard had been defending someone when he'd gotten the scar. Had it been a knife? A jagged piece of glass?

Jamal rubbed his jaw, then commanded, "Yusef, I need to know she'll be safe outside."

Yusef remained stoic and calm, even as he nodded and said, "I'll see to it she returns unharmed."

Jamal stepped back to the gaming table with obvious reluctance. "Make certain you do."

# Chapter Twelve

It was almost a relief to step outside into the peace and quiet, where the whistles and bells of slot machines, and the shouts and disappointed groans of gamblers didn't intrude, and where fresh air replaced perfumes and aftershaves.

Not even the luxury cars that parking attendants whisked away or brought back could detract her from filling her lungs with calming breaths before she pressed the cell phone to her ear.

"Hi, Dad."

"Yasmine, finally. I've been trying to get in touch with you but the honeymoon huts have a strict 'no contact' policy."

"What is so important that you needed to speak to me on my honeymoon?" Her heart jumped. "Is Mom okay?"

"Yes, yes, she's fine," he said brusquely, disregarding his wife like one would disregard a piece of furniture. "The same can't be said for the trade deal I made with your husband."

Her stomach sank to her toes. "What deal *did* you make?"

"I gather your husband doesn't speak to you on matters of finance?"

Her eyes narrowed. Her dad sounded so sanctimonious, like he and Jamal thought alike in that a woman didn't need to discuss men's business. Like women were below men in every way. Had he forgotten about her business and languages degree? "We speak of many things; his finances though are a topic we've yet to discuss."

"Then let me fill you in on the agreement I have with your husband."

She twisted one of her loose strands of hair, her stomach knotting. Whatever her father said it wouldn't be something she'd want to hear.

He hadn't rung because he'd missed her—he wasn't that kind of a dad—he wanted her to do something for him, something that would benefit him while possibly putting her in a compromising position.

"As you know Amack has surplus dates for our needs. Jamal has offered to buy these from us in exchange for much better oil prices. Not only will cheap oil be better for our economy in every way, the dates will give our growers guaranteed income and many workers new jobs

"There's a 'but' in there somewhere."

"But he's asking for many more dates than what we grow. We need to plant thousands more date trees." His voice sharpened. "We can't lose this deal, Yasmine."

"What has any of that got to do with me? Do you want me to explain we can't meet his—"

"No!" He exhaled heavily. "Of course not. I don't want him to lose faith in the deal...in me. We just need a cash injection to begin planting those trees."

Her stomach plummeted, the gold-plated credit card inside her clutch purse suddenly weighing her down. "And let me guess, you want me to send that cash injection to you?"

"I wouldn't have asked Yasmine unless it was important, you know that. Our whole economy relies on this deal."

*Relies on you.*

If she refused her people and country would suffer economic loss, if she agreed she'd be going behind her husband's back, throwing money to her father so soon after he'd already cashed in on a more than generous dowry.

"Let me think about it," she said, her mind as heavy as her heart.

"There's no time for that, Yasmine. You know dates take four to eight years just to produce fruit. We'll have to try and make do with the dates we have until then even if that means having to strip them from our own people."

"You can't do that!"

"I can and I will. This is our only hope, Yasmine. Even the light at the end of the tunnel in regards to tourism is nothing more than a glimmer."

Her mouth dried. "How much do you think you'll need?"

"Nine million dirham should be enough for a start."

"For a start?" she asked weakly.

Jamal might have given her access to unlimited funds, but she'd had no intention of using the card for anything more than an occasional shopping trip. What her dad asked of her was nothing short of insanity. Did he *want* her marriage to fail before it'd even begun?

"Don't play innocent now, Yasmine. You knew when you wed him that you'd be helping your people and your homeland, not to mention your mother. The influx of cash will make her life a whole lot better, too."

Her stomach twisted. Her dad wasn't above using blackmail to get what he wanted. She mightn't care about his opinion but she did care about her mother's wellbeing. He was mean enough to make her mother's life hell if Yasmine didn't fall into line. But what he asked of her would seriously jeopardize her marriage and Jamal's respect of them both.

A sudden breeze rustled the date palms that lined the circular driveway like sentinels, lifting some strands of hair off her nape and cooling her suddenly heated face. "What do you think Jamal will say when he finds out?"

"Oh, he won't be happy, but he has you now, Yasmine. I'm sure you know how to make him forget his anger and the transfer of funds." He chuckled crudely into her ear. "Besides, that money is just a drop in the ocean compared to his real wealth, I'm quite sure he is rich enough to splash some of it my way. My daughter is his wife, after all."

A luxury stretch limousine pulled to a stop in front of the casino. A group of men climbed out of the vehicle, a couple of them leering at her as they stumbled toward the building. She lifted her chin and straightened regally even as her bodyguard stepped out of the shadows behind the brightly lit façade of the casino, a hand on his holster.

One man was too intent on her to notice anyone else. "You look lonely, sweetheart." He grabbed at his crotch. "I know just how to make you feel loved." He guffawed at his own joke before his mouth clapped shut and his eyes widened at finally seeing the huge man who guarded her.

"No offense intended," he mumbled, before he and the other men stammered out apologies and staggered into the casino.

Yasmine nodded and smiled at her bodyguard, her shoulders loosening slightly. She'd never been more thankful for Jamal's insistence to have someone looking out for her in public. A pity the same couldn't be said for her personal life. Her father was a leech capable of sucking blood from a stone.

But if her dad was even aware of the men who'd approached her he didn't let on. He had selective hearing when needed. Instead he continued to reinforce to her how badly the funds were needed before she finally ended the call with, "I'll see what I can do."

# Chapter Thirteen

Jamal was only half-focused on his game. He was too busy observing his wife through the huge glass doors as she stood outside talking on her cell. Even from a distance he noted her taut posture, her body stiffening further when a group of inebriated men piled out of their vehicle before leering at her suggestively.

When one of those same men had the nerve to approach and speak to her, Jamal had already left the gaming table behind along with his stack of chips. He stalked past slot machines and other gaming tables, ignoring the many gamblers to focus on the men entering the casino's huge lobby, their bleary-eyed focus straying back to Yasmine.

They were clearly reluctant just yet to leave her alone.

Jamal approached the man who'd spoken to Yasmine. Grabbing hold of his jacket lapels, he pushed him against the wall. "You dare to make suggestions to my wife—your sheikha!—and treat her with such disrespect?"

The man shrank back and his friends dispersed like rabbits down a warren. He swallowed hard, his drunken state no doubt sharpening as adrenaline surged. "My sincerest apologies Sheikh Jamal, I h-had no idea she w-was your wife. Please forgive me for my mistake."

Though rage continued to burn through him, Jamal resisted throwing a punch at the man and instead released him. Two more of Jamal's bodyguards closed in to assist him, and he waved them back to focus on the now sober man in front of him. "Perhaps next time you might treat a woman with the respect she deserves."

"Of c-course, you're right Sheikh Jamal, m-my profound apologies. It won't ever happen again."

Jamal exhaled harshly, his hands fisting at his sides. "Then go—*now*, before I change my mind and make you pay for your vile insult."

The man took off running and disappeared into the crowd, no doubt hoping to become just another anonymous face.

Jamal wouldn't ever forget him.

He shook his head. He had better things to focus on now. He continued toward the glass entrance doors and they opened silently as he stalked through them, stepping outside just as Yasmine ended her call to her dad. Cocking his head to the side, Jamal repeated, "You'll see what you can do?"

She started at his voice, then laughed shakily. "Jamal, I didn't see you there."

"I wanted to make sure you were okay."

Her voice cracked and she averted her gaze. "Of course I am, why wouldn't I be?"

"You mean aside from those intoxicated men, one of whom appeared to harass you?"

She blinked as she looked back at him. "You don't miss much, do you?"

He stepped closer. "Did they frighten you?"

She shook her head. "No, your security scared them off."

He nodded at the security man who'd faded back discreetly the moment Jamal had approached. "Good work, Yusef. I'll see to it you get a bonus."

Yusef bowed. "It's my honor, Sheikh Jamal."

Jamal drew his wife against him, breathing in her delicious vanilla and freesia fragrance. The back of her gown featured a cutout heart-shape, and he ran one of his hands along her bared skin while his other hand cupped her butt.

That she was trembling detracted him from anything deeper though than concern. He drew back and looked down at her, her blue eyes wary as she lifted her head to hold his gaze.

"You're shaking," he said gently. "If those men did or said anything to offend you—"

"No, they were harmless enough. I think they were more scared of Yusef than I was of them."

"So your father's phone call upset you?"

*"Every* talk I have with my dad upsets me."

His protective instincts arose, blocking out common sense when he growled, "Then perhaps it's better to cut communication with him."

Pink flushed her face. "You can't control me, Jamal, not like that. He's my father whether I like it or not. I can't have you dictate who I can and can't talk to."

He nodded stiffly. *Shit.* He was probably reminding him of her father and that was the last thing he wanted. But he refused to see her hurt, too. "I don't want to take away your freedom, Yasmine. I simply don't want to see you upset by anyone. That includes your dad. If he has said anything to you I should know about—"

"No." She shook her head, her eyes shadowed. "It was nothing." She pasted on a bright smile. "What I am right now is starving, and I did see a wonderful restaurant inside."

He crooked his arm, though his heart was heavy. She was hiding something from him. "Well then, let's eat."

# Chapter Fourteen

Yasmine surreptitiously watched her husband as he read the menu, her own menu in front of her face as she pretended to do the same thing.

He looked up and caught her staring, and he grinned and asked, "How does steak tartare sound?"

She resisting an emphatic shake of her head and telling him raw meat wasn't her thing, no matter that the citrus gently cooked it. But thanks to her dad, staying agreeable and polite to Jamal was in her best interest now.

She didn't want her marriage wrecked before it'd even begun, yet that was exactly what might happen if she kept giving into her dad's demands.

*What other choice do you have? Your people need you, too.*

It didn't make her any less sick to the stomach having to go through with it.

The waiter arrived and Jamal ordered their steak tartare and a bottle of champagne. The chilled bubbly was brought to them minutes later and Jamal poured them each a glass, then raised his flute in a toast. "To us," he announced.

She lifted her own glass, then added, "May our marriage be a long and happy one."

His gaze turned speculative as they *clinked* their glasses together and drank deep. Her stomach roiled again. But if he suspected something he didn't bring it up, instead they talked about neutral subjects until the waiter arrived with their dinner.

Yasmine hid a grimace at the compressed round of meat with capers and herbs, and topped with a raw egg yolk. She swallowed hard as she picked up her fork, spearing a piece of the meat dressed with lemon juice and some of the egg yolk before she took a delicate mouthful. The meat was tender and no doubt tasty, but she had serious trouble swallowing it.

She played with her food for a handful of minutes while Jamal ate his with gusto. Then placing her fork onto the side of her plate, she leaned back in her seat and pushed her plate away. Forcing herself to eat anymore would make her stomach rebel further.

Jamal dabbed at one corner of his mouth with a napkin. "Are you not enjoying your meal?"

"It was...lovely. But I've had enough."

He cocked a brow. "You've barely eaten more than a mouthful."

Her husband was far too observant. She was beginning to resent how he noticed absolutely everything and nothing got past him. Her father wouldn't have cared less if she picked at her food like a sparrow. Perhaps that was why her dad was flailing while Jamal was so successful.

Next time she'd order what she wanted.

"Steak tartare possibly wasn't the best choice for me," she conceded.

"Oh?"

She ran her finger along the gold edge of her plate. "I usually enjoy my steak well-done."

His brows lowered. "Then why didn't you say so?" He raised his arm and a waiter hurried over. "Can we exchange this steak tartare for your finest piece of steak, cooked well-done."

"Of course, Sheikh Jamal," the waiter said, his voice shaking with nerves. He clearly had a serious case of hero worship. "Would there be anything else with the steak?"

Jamal glanced at Yasmine and she smiled and said, "Chips and salad please, and pepper gravy on the steak." She cleared her throat. "I have a hankering for some old fashioned pub food."

The waiter nodded and whisked away her steak tartare before he placed her new order at the restaurant counter.

Jamal sipped his champagne. "You know, I don't expect you to indulge me by eating what I eat. You're safe to be your true self with me."

Her pulse thudded in her ears. He really was too perceptive. She managed an idle shrug and held his stare. "I used to hate avocado once, I love it now. My palate is ever changing. Clearly not with raw meat, though."

He leaned back in his seat. "It is an acquired taste."

Yasmine nodded. "So I've found." She took another sip of her champagne before pushing her chair back and standing. "If you'll excuse me for a moment, I have need of the ladies room."

Jamal pushed to his feet, then nodded at one of his security staff to follow her.

"That's really not necessary," she protested.

"My men are discreet, I promise." He held her gaze. "He'll wait outside just as a precaution. We can't be too careful outside the palace."

She sighed. "I don't know why I assumed I'd have more freedom once I was married."

Jamal's smile looked more apologetic than amused. "It will be quite the reverse, I'm afraid. We're a rich nation and there are many who covet what we have, which makes you the perfect target to acquire as a bargaining chip."

She shivered at his words, before she mumbled something about not taking too long and hurrying out of the restaurant. It was a relief to get to the ladies room, where she sat on the lid of one of the many empty toilets while taking out her credit card and taking photos with her cell phone of the credit card numbers and security code before sending the images off to her dad.

She had no idea if there was a maximum amount she could transfer at a time but she had no doubt her dad and his accountant would find a way to withdraw the necessary sum. She'd just have to find a way to deal with the fallout.

She pressed a hand to her brow and sighed heavily. She couldn't lie to Jamal any longer. She'd have to broach the subject with him once they were back at the honeymoon hut. But not now, she refused to ruin their night out.

# Chapter Fifteen

Yasmine glanced out the jeep window to the many city lights shining outside. She glanced up high, but the glaring artificial lights made it near impossible to make out the starry heavens above.

She used to love sitting on Amack's palace rooftop to look up at the stars, they appeared so close it was as if she could touch them. Now it was as if her marriage was as tantalizingly close yet just out of reach.

A shiver went down her spine. Jamal wouldn't deal well with her betrayal.

He drove his car through the resort gates, the lighting that hit the tops of the palms and the gateway itself much more subdued and intimate. At least there was no need for garish lighting here. Even the apartment buildings emitted a soft glow that was serene and calming, the beauty of the resort speaking for itself.

A pity she was anything but relaxed. Her heart beat erratically in her chest, the adrenaline that pumped through her body ratcheting up her tension.

Jamal parked the car in front of their honeymoon hut, where solar lights gleamed faintly at the front and along the railing of the boardwalk, throwing out just enough light for guidance to the front door. Jamal opened her door and she took his proffered hand as she got out and took in a deep, steadying breath of the crisp, briny air as the sea gently lapped at the shore and the boardwalk posts.

But it was like she was having an outer body experience, watching as if a spectator looking from the outside in at a series of preordained events about to unfold.

She sensed Jamal's scrutiny as they walked across the boardwalk. How much longer would he want to touch her? She only wished the cool night air gave her flushed skin and guilty countenance some relief.

She glanced at the security team who'd stayed well back from them. They stood outside their silenced cars, no doubt checking the shadows for any movement until she and Jamal had safely entered their hut.

A motion sensor light flicked on as they stepped into the hut, Jamal sliding the lock into place on the front door before he looked at her. "Are you okay? You haven't been yourself since your dad's phone call."

Now was the perfect time to tell him the truth. Except she had no idea how far Jamal could be pushed before he'd react. She looked away. He'd believe she was not only untrustworthy and weak, but a gold digger, too. Traits he'd despise in a wife.

He clasped her chin, drawing her gaze back to his. "Yasmine, what is it you're hiding?"

She swallowed hard. She couldn't lie to him, not anymore. He deserved the truth no matter the consequences. She opened her mouth just as a heavy tread on the boardwalk was followed by a knock on the front door.

He frowned, annoyed by the interruption. But then his frown turned to concern, realizing right along with Yasmine and her sinking stomach that whoever knocked it could only be for something important. "Who is it?" he barked.

"It's Yusef. Sorry to interrupt you Sheikh Jamal, but you have an urgent phone call."

Yasmine's nerves twanged hard, and she reached helplessly for her husband as he turned and unlocked the door. Her arm dropped back to her side and she stood paralyzed as he put the cell to his ear and conversed with the caller on the other end. Even in her numb state it didn't take her long to decipher the call was from his financial advisor.

Her dad had obviously found a way to transfer the huge sum of money in record time. He hadn't wanted to take the chance she'd change her mind and tell her husband the truth.

She still hadn't moved when Jamal ended the call. His face as tight as his shoulders, he said nothing as he handed the phone back to Yusef and closed the door firmly back in place.

Her nerves stretched to breaking point, she said weakly, "Before you say anything, I'm truly sorry."

"Are you?" his voice throbbed with censure. "The money in that account was for you, Yasmine, *not* your father. Why didn't you talk to me? Why hide the truth? Did you seriously think I wouldn't find out about it coming out of my account?"

"I was scared and ashamed," she whispered, her throat drier than parchment. "I didn't know what to do. Dad said we needed to plant thousands more date palms to meet your demands and that our people were relying on me—"

"The same people who have survived perfectly well without any extra influx of cash for the last few years?" he interjected harshly. "As for the date palms, don't you think I would have fully investigated every aspect of my new business venture before going ahead with it? Your country has more than enough dates for my needs and for your people."

She blinked, her heart stuttering. "Are you saying my dad lied to me?"

Jamal's jaw tightened, but there was a shadow of sympathy in his stare.

She blinked back sudden tears. She didn't know what was worse, her dad's betrayal or her husband's sympathy when she'd been expecting nothing but his well-deserved wrath.

It showed how little she knew him still...knew her dad.

"I'd hoped to soften the blow when I told you, but there's no longer any way of skirting around the truth. Your father is a gambling addict who has probably already frittered away half the money you sent him.

Amack would have held its own even with its failing tourism if it wasn't for your father's secret addiction."

"I don't believe you!"

"Yes, you do," he said quietly, his brilliant eyes reading her emotions. She was an open book to him. "His racehorses aren't winning like they used to and yet he still gambles heavily on them. Now you, his only daughter, is expected to pick up the pieces of his broken dreams."

She didn't realize she was crying at first, not until Jamal reached out and dried her tears with his thumbs. "Angel, don't cry." He sighed heavily. "All I ask it that the next time your dad asks for money, you come to me first."

She must have nodded, because he scooped her up in his arms and carried her into to the bedroom. Laying her onto the bed, he pressed kisses to each corner of her eyes, drying her tears as effectively as his hands had. "I only want you to be happy," he said huskily

"I only want you to be happy, too."

"Angel, I've never been happier than I am when I'm with you."

Heaven help her, but her husband undid her in every way. Despite what she'd done he knew all the right things to say. "You're too good to me," she whispered.

He pressed a kiss to her parted lips. "Marriage takes work." He kissed her jawline next. "And commitment." Then he was trailing kisses down the side of her neck, where inner sparks danced and heated. "And I happen to think you're worth it," he finished simply.

How did his words break her apart and bare her heart so easily? That he meant every one of them left her speechless while her body hummed with arousal and need.

But she didn't need to tell him when her body communicated it so well. She lifted her hips and then her shoulders as he peeled off her dress and underwear. His eyes glowed and he growled something illegible as he drew the tip of first one breast into his mouth, then the other.

She arched her back with a gasp. How soon her aching misery had become aching need. She wanted her husband in every way. That she'd failed his trust tore at her heartstrings and turned her yearning bittersweet.

"Don't think," Jamal commanded huskily. "Just enjoy the moment."

She *was* enjoying it, very much.

It was time to show him. She rolled and suddenly he was underneath and she was on top. "I want to pleasure you," she said huskily.

His eyes darkened. "If this is your way of making up for—"

"I want you, Jamal. But I want to be in control." She didn't need to tell him that though every aspect of her life was taken over by rules and security, the bedroom was the one place where she could enact her own needs.

He nodded and his cock jerked beneath her. "Then I'm all yours."

It was beyond intimate to pull off his clothes and bare his skin like he'd bared hers. Beyond seductive being in control when she bent and pressed her lips to his and dragged her soaked pussy along his satin-hard shaft.

His cock kicked and he growled into her mouth, his pleasure setting loose her an assurance and self-confidence she never knew she possessed.

"I want to be inside you," he said harshly, his eyes flared and his cock pulsating beneath her.

She again dragged her inviting wetness along his length, her words pausing between each back and forth motion. "Not. Until. I. Say. So."

His eyes lit up even as a muscle jerked into life at one side of his jaw. "You really are perfect in every way."

She moaned and tilted her hips forward as she rocked on him, her engorged clit soaking up the heated friction until she was dripping wet and an orgasm tore through her. She cried out at the blast of sensation, collapsing over Jamal as she convulsed again and again with pleasure.

She was only half-aware of Jamal rolling her back underneath him before he slammed inside her, stroking hard and fast until he too succumbed with a roar, his seed filling her.

She was still panting when he tenderly brushed the hair back from her face and kissed her with slow restraint. She sighed luxuriously against his mouth, caught up in the whirlwind of feelings and emotions. She could so completely and utterly fall for him.

A pang went through her heart. She was halfway there already.

Who wouldn't fall for such a dynamic, charismatic man? He was a great leader, compassionate but ruthless when needed. Little wonder his people loved him.

"What are you thinking about?" he murmured, his eyes heavy-lidded and his body relaxed and warm against hers.

"Not what, *who,*" she said with a smile.

"Dare I hope that who is me?"

"I don't know if I should admit it," she returned, her smile growing. "I don't want your head to swell."

"Which head are we talking about?" he asked with a little smirk.

She giggled. "Definitely not the one that was so swollen it exploded."

His chuckle reverberated through her and left her whole body tingling, not helped at all when he nuzzled her ear and added goose bumps to the mix.

"Next time we make love it'll be for hours and I'll give you multiple orgasms. Then I'll lick and suck you to give you more."

He carefully disconnected from her and lay on his side, pulling her so that she faced him. "We're good together, angel. Never forget that." His lashes were sliding shut when he muttered thickly, "You'll make a wonderful mother to our children."

# Chapter Sixteen

Yasmine woke with a smile on her face and stickiness between her thighs. Sometime during the night Jamal must have swathed them both under a bedcover, as she was almost too deliciously cozy and warm now.

She breathed in the sexy scent of sandalwood and cinnamon, all too aware her husband was next to her even before she turned to look at him in the faint dawn light coming through the window. Her smile widened. He'd shown his stamina last night and was now clearly sated and sound asleep. Even with his designer stubble close to becoming a beard and covering half his face, his unguarded features looked softer, more youthful.

It was impossible to believe sometimes he was twelve years older than her twenty years, and had accomplished so much. She must seem so young and naïve. Little wonder he was shocked by her deception. She was only surprised he hadn't taken the credit card away from her.

She slipped out of bed and walked naked into the bathroom. Stepping into the shower, she turned on the taps and allowed the hot water to stream over her aching, tired body. Jamal hadn't been joking when he said they'd make love for hours. But though her body was sore, the pleasure had made it more than worthwhile.

Her husband had never been so open and loving, his feelings for her transparent. He adored her, maybe even loved her. Her heart wrenched. How could he possibly love her after what she'd done? After all, love went hand-in-hand with trust and she'd blown that by giving into her father's demands.

Not that Jamal had used her culpability against her. She'd expected outrage at the very least, but he'd shown quite the opposite. She only hoped her returned devotion was enough for him.

After washing her hair, she towel dried and brushed it while studying her reflection in the mirror. Her eyes were bright, her cheeks flushed and her lips plumped and thoroughly kissed. She didn't look like a wife who'd sinned, she looked radiant and happy.

Not even guilt could overshadow her joy. For the first time in her life she wasn't constantly worried about putting a foot wrong. As a sheikha she was constantly self-aware. What she wore, how she acted, what she said...

With Jamal she felt safe. Relaxed. That he was quick to forgive and not hold grudges made her appreciate him on a whole new level.

Stepping into the walk-in robe, she pulled on a pink sundress and a pretty pair of sandals before strolling back into the bedroom. Her husband was still asleep, but he'd kicked aside the covers and lay on his stomach with his ass and strong thighs exposed, giving her quite the view.

She refrained from touching him, and instead retrieved her clutch purse before going into the kitchen and pouring a glass of juice. Taking out her birth control pills, she popped one free and stared at it in her palm while Jamal's words repeated like a mantra in her head.

*You'll make a wonderful mother to our children.*

Did she want that now, too? She wasn't so sure anymore. Knowing his feelings for her were strong and real made her second-guess everything.

*Don't be an idiot. You'll be a mom when you're one hundred percent certain it's what you want.*

She popped the pill and drank it down with her juice.

"What are you doing?"

Jamal's sleep-roughened voice made her jump guiltily, her elbow hitting the foil packet of birth control pills and making them skitter across the kitchen counter and onto the floor.

She was frozen as he stalked forward and picked them up, his face at first incredulous than darkening with sick rage. "Why the hell are you taking these?"

She trembled. He was angrier at this than the millions she'd allowed her dad to withdraw from Jamal's bank account. "I-I'm not ready to be a mother."

"And you didn't think to tell me that when we agreed on the marriage?" He shook his head, his face grief-stricken and hollow. "What did I ever do to you to make you lie to me?" He stepped back, his eyes hard and his mouth tight. "You know what, I don't want to know. I don't want to hear your excuses. I don't even want to look at you."

Grief hit like a sledgehammer. "You don't mean that."

His gaze glittered. "Oh, but I do. You're no angel. You're the devil in disguise. I just wished I'd seen it sooner."

She blinked, confused by his sudden shift toward her. "It's my body, my choice."

"It's *our* choice!" he shouted, his face blanching of all color. "Having children was all I wanted from you."

A punch to her stomach couldn't have brought her any more pain. "At least now I know the truth," she whispered.

His fists clenching at his sides, he said bitterly, "I knew you were hiding something from me. But I had no idea you'd stoop *this* low. You betrayed me more than you could possibly know."

"I've delayed having a family. I don't see what the big deal—"

*"Don't."* He exhaled roughly. "I can't hear your excuses. I can't deal with them...with *you* right now."

She gaped as he pivoted and pulled open the front door, slamming it shut behind him as he stepped outside. But she was too shocked to go after him. Too shocked to do anything but stare blankly at the closed door.

But finally realization set in. This was it then...the end of her marriage. She had to admit it'd been ideal while it had lasted. Too bad she'd been completely wrong about her husband having feelings for her. He'd only ever been interested in her bloodline for their future children.

She sucked in a quivery breath. She'd been delusional in thinking he'd actually cared about her. He cared only about her being a mother to his progeny.

She retrieved her birth control pills. How had something so innocuous destroyed her marriage?

*It's not just about the pills. You betrayed him yet again.*

She crumpled the packet in her hand before tossing them aside. There was more to his anger than that, she was certain of it. She'd exposed a nerve, uncovered an underlying emotion she'd probably never see again.

She dragged a hand over her face, suddenly suffocated by anxiety. She needed some fresh air. She stepped out onto the back sundeck where the lap pool beckoned. She ignored it and went down a dozen steps to the lower level where private jet skis were moored.

That had been today's planned activity, and she'd been really looking forward to it.

Removing her sandals, she sat at the edge of the planks with a heavy sigh, her feet sinking into the water as she gazed sightlessly into the horizon of endless blue.

She'd thought her marriage with Jamal might actually work. That he'd been so good to her, so forgiving had planted tendrils of hope deep into her soul. Those same tendrils were already beginning to wither and die.

As a sheikha she didn't have a lot of options. She was expected to marry someone important, have a load of children and stay in the background where she played her role as respectful wife and mother.

That she'd started to see her role with Jamal in a far nicer light was to her own detriment. She'd imagined love and romance, but all he'd ever seen in her was a womb to carry their children.

She was so lost in thought she didn't at first hear the speedboat approaching. Only as it got closer did she look up and see it coming her way. She stood, and about to back away, she saw Yusef in the boat. She exhaled with a bitter, little laugh, then lifted a hand and waved.

She had nothing to fear with her bodyguard nearby.

Yusef nodded, but was otherwise too busy grabbing hold of the nearest wooden post to keep the boat from colliding with the lower deck. Only once the boat was secured did he jump onto the deck with Yasmine.

She cocked her head to the side. "Did Jamal send you?" Her chest warmed. If so surely that meant he still cared about her? "As you can see, I'm perfectly safe."

Yusef gave her a pained look, then pinched the bridge of his nose and closed his eyes. "I regret to tell you that you are indeed in danger, Sheikha Yasmine."

Her heart did an extra beat. "Whatever do you—"

Yusef clapped a hand over her mouth and dragged her roughly against him. At first she went limp, shocked to the core. Yusef was the bad guy! He lifted her against his chest like she weighed nothing, then jumped back into the boat.

She struggled wildly, but it was too little too late, and he was too damn strong. It didn't stop her from chomping on his hand and drawing blood, the coppery taste filling her mouth.

He grunted and threw her to the floor of the boat. Pain exploded through her ribs and her skull as she landed heavily against the edge of a seat, dizziness for a moment keeping her still.

Before she even tried to clamber to her feet, the boat had powered off, away from the honeymoon hut...away from Jamal and any chance she'd had of staying with him.

# Chapter Seventeen

Jamal had long finished the phone call to the PI when he strode back into the honeymoon hut, his heart heavy. Damn it! He'd let his emotion rules his head and he'd hurt Yasmine along the way.

His wife had been falling for him, he'd been certain of it, but he'd jeopardized all that now and was back to square one again, any progress with her null and void.

He'd seriously fucked up.

His past had never been Yasmine's burden to bear. He alone had to live with the baby he'd lost, his son who'd died before he'd even taken his first breath. Not only had his stillborn baby been lifeless, he'd never even been given a name.

That alone had nearly broken him.

But Takisha, the mother of his stillborn child, had refused to name him and Jamal had given her that small mercy. Instead he'd focused on giving his son a decent burial and someplace nice for Takisha to live. He also sent her a monthly allowance that enabled her to live a rich and fulfilling life.

That his generosity made her fancy herself in love with him was in no way reciprocated by him. Those feelings belonged exclusively to his wife...if she hadn't already left him.

Perhaps that was why his pulse thudded on finding the hut empty, the packet of birth control pills mocking him from where they lay crumpled on the kitchen floor. He stalked out to the deck, the pool shining like a beacon while the dread in his belly escalated. "Yasmine!"

The quiet mocked him as he ran down the stairs to the lower deck and pier. At finding the pair of delicate women's sandals near the edge of the deck, his heart cramped painfully. He scooped the sandals up, his stomach hitting rock bottom as he imagined the worst and scanned the water for her.

Dropping the sandals, he dragged off his jacket and shoes. About to dive into the ocean, a tread on the upper deck made him pause. His heart in his throat, he raced back upstairs, his pulse jackhammering, then missing a beat at finding one of his security men standing there.

Jamal's eyes narrowed. "Tell me you know where Yasmine is."

"She's missing?"

Jamal swallowed down sick rage. "Yes, she's damn well missing!"

The man shuffled his feet nervously, then explained, "I'm sorry to hear that, Sheikh Jamal. I'm here because Yusef has also disappeared."

# Chapter Eighteen

Yasmine wiggled her fingers, doing her best to relieve the numbness from them. But ever since Yusef had tied her arms tightly behind her back, there was barely any feeling left in her arms or hands.

She was only glad they hadn't gagged her. Not that there was anyone around to hear her screams for help. The ocean was deserted, as was the beach they were headed toward, with sand dunes marching back into a desert as far as the eye could see.

She swallowed hard. Were they going to kill her? Or where these same people going to trade her back to Jamal for money?

She looked at her captors, memorizing them.

Not that she'd ever forget Yusef. To think she'd trusted the man! She should have listened to her instincts. Now the scar that ran through one side of his beard looked ominous, not intriguing. Even his eyes appeared flatter, meaner, his lips pressed into a hard, unforgiving line.

The other two men were as dissimilar as could be. The one who sat at the stern of the boat and steering the vessel was short and as thick as a barrel, his fleshy face showing no emotion whatsoever. The other who sat at the bow in a seat in front of her was a tall, reed-thin man with a swarthy, pockmarked face and eyes that constantly moved around, his hands twitching and his demeanor highly-strung and nervous.

"Algo no se siente bien en esto," the tall man muttered.

She smiled grimly as she deciphered his words. "That's because nothing good will come out of this."

His head swiveled quickly, his eyes bugging out as though on strings. "You speak Spanish."

She nodded. Thanks to having a number of foreign nannies and maids, even before her studies she'd had a knack for other languages. "I do."

Yusef glowered at Yasmine, then pointed to the bloodied strip of material he'd wrapped around his hand, the same one she'd bitten. "Open your mouth again and I will shove this filthy rag inside it."

She resisted glowering right back at him and instead dropped her eyes. The idea of the bloody gag in her mouth made her stomach churn in queasy protest. With any luck she'd said enough to nurture the seed of doubt already sprouting in the tall man's mind.

Blood began to drip through the cloth on Yusef's hand, splattering the gray, marine-grade carpet beneath. He didn't look concerned. He was beginning to look excited, anticipating whatever was ahead.

Her stomach knotted. It couldn't be a good thing, not for her.

Whatever was in store for her wouldn't be pleasant. She was either their ticket to a better life, or a way to derail Jamal and make him suffer for whatever sins he might have committed against someone.

She swallowed hard, and forced herself to at least try and get some answers. Looking up at Yusef, she asked, "Can I at least ask where you are taking me?"

He shrugged. "What does it matter? You'll get what you deserve now."

She held back tears. No doubt Yusef and the other men would enjoy seeing her scared. "And what *do* I deserve?"

He snorted. "You humiliated and betrayed Sheikh Arif. You deserve whatever punishment he devises."

Horror for a moment stole away her breath. Out of all the reasons for getting kidnapped that one hadn't even crossed her mind. Better to get shot in the head than endure whatever Arif had planned. "Do you have any idea what he does to women, and most especially to his enemies? He will tear me apart piece-by-piece."

Though Yusef for a moment looked uncomfortable, he lifted his bloodied hand with a scowl and shook his head. "You're lucky I didn't hurt you after what you did to me."

"Why didn't you?" she asked bitterly.

"Why?" Yusef chuckled. "Because Sheikh Arif wants you unscathed and unharmed. He wants to have all the pleasure in hurting you. And hurt you he will."

Calmness was about as far out of reach as her husband was from her now. "You won't get away with this! Jamal will kill every one of you to get to me."

Yusef threw his head back and laughed. "Do you really think he'll care what happens to you after what you did?"

She blinked. "How do you know—"

He snorted and she froze, her stomach hardening. "You had the room wired, didn't you?"

Of course he did. He'd been the first one to go inside the honeymoon hut and ensure it was safe. It had been the perfect opportunity for him to plant the necessary devices that enabled him to hear their every conversation...and more.

He nodded and smirked. "I did. It was rather interesting hearing your conversations. It was even more interesting hearing the both of you in bed. I should probably thank you. Your sexual performances had me jacking off more times than I can count."

The short man snorted, and she glanced back to find him staring at her with a glint in his eyes and a leer on his face. But clearly he took the "no touch" rule seriously and stayed in his seat.

Yet despite the men's distance and the relentless heat, she shivered. If she'd been scared to marry Sheikh Arif, she was terrified of what he'd do to her now thanks to her rejection. Compared to Arif, these men were nothing more than trained dogs.

She glanced wildly between them. "Whatever Arif has offered, Jamal will double it!"

Yusef laughed. "Nice try. But you know as well as us that he will kill us all if we're stupid enough to get caught. And we are most definitely not stupid."

The short man leaned forward in his seat. "What we *are* is desperate for payment. Which means we'll take your wedding and engagement rings."

Yasmine glanced down at her rings. They were a part of her now. Perhaps the only comfort she'd have in the coming days. "They're mine," she gritted out.

Yusef frowned at the shorter man. "Not a good idea, Odai."

Odai's eyes gleamed. "They will be worth a small fortune. Why not take what we can from this deal? No one would begrudge us a bonus. We'll split the profits three ways once we sell them."

Yusef didn't say anything as small waves pushed the speedboat toward the shore. Odai reduced the motor to idle until they were in waist deep water. The taller, now silent man put down an anchor and Odai switched off the engine.

Yasmine didn't take much notice of what happened after that. She was aware only of Odai then capturing her bound wrists and prying the rings off her finger. She struggled and cried out, but there was absolutely nothing she could do with her arms tied behind her back.

She was just grateful that there were no jewels in her lobes. She'd made it a habit to take off her earrings before bed. Odai didn't share her sentiments. At her lack of jewelry he cuffed her across the head, leaving her ears ringing and her head aching.

"Don't hurt her," Yusef growled. "Do you want to face the wrath of Sheikh Arif?"

Odai pocketed the rings and shrugged. "You betrayed Sheikh Jamal. I'd be more concerned about *his* plans of retribution."

Yusef's face whitened. "Jamal will come after all of us, not just me. We have to be smart from here on in and not get noticed. Selling the Sheikha's rings will put us right under the spotlight."

The taller man finally spoke, his voice now firm and resolute, as though he'd made his mind up he was in this all the way. "Then you get to walk away without the bonus sale of the rings. Either way, Sheikh Jamal's focus will be on finding you. By the time he does, Odai and I will have long disappeared, never to be found."

Odai chuckled at his friend's sudden grit, then nodded toward the beach. "Here they are."

Yasmine followed his gaze and cringed at seeing the handful of camels plodding toward them from the desert, their riders then commanding their steeds to kneel next to the ocean.

Whatever Yusef might have said next was cast aside as he focused on the riders at the beach and said with a heartless smile, "Time to go."

# Chapter Nineteen

Yasmine held back panic as Yusef picked her up and held her against his chest. *Ugh,* how she would love to add to the scar that cut through his beard. But as he slipped from the boat into the water and waded toward shore, attacking him was impossible, not with her arms tied. She was more concerned about drowning if he released her.

It was only once they reached the sandy shore, where she caught sight of Sheikh Arif, that panic morphed into terror. His age didn't make him any less threatening. His lifeless dark eyes pierced right through her, his thin mouth, fat jowls and hooked nose making her think of a predator about to swoop for its prey.

It didn't mean she'd submit to him. Once Yusef set her onto her feet, she straightened to her full height. She wasn't tall but she had to be damn near as tall as Arif! She threw back her shoulders. It mattered little that the angle made the ropes burn into her skin. She'd be in far more pain shortly anyway.

Arif stalked toward Yasmine, his white robes scraping along the sand and his nut-brown eyes glittering. "I should have known you'd be dressed like a western woman. A slut." He nodded to Yusef. "Cut off her ropes. I didn't want her bruised or hurt."

Yusef nodded, then used a serrated knife to cut through her bindings. She bit her lower lip at the drag and pull motion that teared at her skin. When the rope finally broke and fell away, there was no relief. Though her arms moved freely, her now flowing blood sent pins and needles coursing through her veins.

She refused to cry out in pain, refused to cower in any way. These men would enjoy that far too much.

Arif stopped right in front of her, inspecting his prize from head to toe. "You were my property, forbidden to marry anyone else but me." Reaching for her hand, he lifted it and asked, "And yet your fingers are bare?"

She didn't respond, and he shoved his face closer to hers, his breath a pungent scent of onions and red wine. "Why *is* that?" he asked.

It took everything she had not to recoil and empty her stomach all over his pudgy, sandaled feet.

It was Yusef who finally broke the strained silence. "Odai took them. He and his partner were planning to sell them."

The tallest of her kidnappers jerked his head toward Yusef, his eyes popping wide open with guilt and panic and his mouth flailing, though no words emerged.

He should have listened to his instincts.

Odai did all the babbling. "My apologies, Sheikh Arif. We intended to give you those rings along with your hostage." He stuck his hand into his robe's pocket, then held the rings in the palm of his hand. "They're yours."

Arif's cold and deadly eyes narrowed, reminding her of some reptilian creature as he stared at Odai. "Why not just leave them on her fingers for me to remove when I wanted them?"

When Odai seemed to lose the power of speech, Arif pulled a gun out of his pocket. *Bang.* He shot the tall man in the head, his lifeless body dropping onto the sand with a *thud.*

"I don't like traitors." When he turned the muzzle toward Odai, he put his hands up, the rings dropping onto the sand. "Please, let me explain, I—"

*Bang.*

Odai dropped dead beside his partner-in-crime, never to get up again, and all of Yasmine's screams stayed on the inside. Arif killed without thought, like taking the life of another human being was as simple as snipping the head off a flower.

Though she didn't condone what the men had done, they might well have families, brothers, sisters, wives, perhaps even innocent children to take care of.

*And what about you? Did they care what Arif would do to you?*

Yusef barely looked at the dead men. "I deeply regret that they tried to cheat you out of what was rightfully yours, Sheikh Arif."

Arif sighed heavily and crossed his arms as he focused on Yusef. "It really is hard to find good help these days." He nodded toward the bodies. "See that you bury them in the dunes."

"I don't have anything to dig—"

"You have hands do you not?" Arif smiled. "A shallow burial will be fine, enough so that they are concealed from human eyes for the next few days. The predators will eventually dig up their remains anyway until nothing but bones are scattered far across the desert."

Yusef bowed consent. "Then it will be done, Sheikh Arif."

Arif's smile widened. "Take the rings as a gesture of goodwill, and do with them what you like. It matters little to me." He looked at Yasmine. "I have all I want right here."

Yusef immediately retrieved the rings and put them in his pocket, and Yasmine's lip curled. He was no better than the men who'd died for a bit of extra cash. No, he was worse! Not only had he sacrificed two lives to save his own, he'd gladly accepted the bonus of her rings. She only hoped his selfishness and greed would be his undoing.

Arif casually pointed his gun at Yasmine. "Now that is all settled, we're going for a ride. I *did* entertain the thought of having you dragged behind one of the camels, but I thought better of it and instead brought a camel for you to ride." His smile gave her no warmth. "I have other plans for you."

She shivered. She didn't want to think about what those plans might be. Instead she asked, "What of my father and my husband—"

*Slap.*

She hadn't even seen Arif's hand move. She hadn't seen it coming at all. But her ears rang and warmth trickled from one nostril. She didn't cry or tremble in front of him. She simply waited while he gathered his composure back around him like a cloak.

"You will never speak to me of their names again. They betrayed me. And now *you* will be the one to pay the price."

As far as Arif was concerned, she was a lowly woman, not in charge of her own destiny. Which mean it hadn't been her decision to marry Jamal instead of Arif. That choice had been entirely up to her father and husband.

Arif stepped behind her and shoved her roughly toward the camels. "Get on."

She blinked at the lone camel kneeling behind the rest of the herd. Even its saddle was old and worn. That Arif expected her to ride a camel in a sundress didn't surprise her. He'd delight in the fact she had nothing to cover her skin from chafing or sunburn, along with no hat, not even a hijab to protect her face.

But she didn't argue, that would be a foolhardy and pointless exercise. She walked stiffly toward the camel, all too aware of the other robed men's stares that gleamed with hostility.

Her throat dried even as the sun pulsed down. What she'd do for a drink of water. She managed to climb awkwardly onto the saddle, the men guffawing and the camel bellowing rejection.

She'd probably flashed them in her dress. She lifted her chin. Let them laugh. She was certain she'd be humiliated a whole lot worse in the coming days.

*If you survive that long.*

# Chapter Twenty

Yasmine had given up trying to keep the sun off her face. She must have sat on the camel now for three or four hours at least, the heat blistering her skin and cracking her lips, while the men laughed and joked as they drank from their water skins and never once offered her a sip.

Jamal had been right. Riding a camel really was nothing short of torture. The jerky, rocking motion had surely taken off half the skin on the inside of her thighs, while her back ached unforgivably as she grew more and more tense the closer they got to their destination.

What was Arif planning for her? A merciless death would be better than whatever slow and torturous scheme he had in mind. She looked down from the height of the camel. Was it high enough to end it all fast if she fell headfirst? No. The chances of dying from a broken neck were slim to none, and her punishment would no doubt escalate for daring to even consider it.

She blinked her gritty eyes, though one was pretty much swollen shut from where Arif had hit her, her top lip sore and puffy, too.

*Huh.* She hurt all over. But she'd bet it'd be a picnic compared to whatever was in store for her. She held back a sob about the same time they crested a sand dune and a spread of colorful tents was laid out below them.

Arif turned to her. "Welcome to your new home, Sheikha Yasmine." He said her name with a curled lip. "How does it feel knowing we are still in Ishmat—*your* home soil now—and yet you're as far away from your husband as you're ever likely to be?"

She managed to shrug. "Jamal will find me."

Arif's eyes burned through her. "What did I say about you ever speaking his name again?"

"You're going to kill me anyway, so what do I care?" she said, her dry, raspy voice barely legible.

Arif seemed to understand though, his eyes glinting with sick delight as he said slyly, "Ah, but there are many ways to kill a person. If you cooperate I can end it fast. If you don't, your pain will be agonizing, intolerable. Now...I'd much prefer to see you suffer, but the level of suffering is all up to you."

She knew deep down he'd make her suffer no matter what she did or said. Saving her bone-dry throat the bother of an answer, she instead slumped in her saddle and ignored him, while trying not to imagine the worst.

But what if Jamal really did find her? He might hate her right now but he was nothing if not honorable. He wouldn't want her death on his conscience. She was his wife and therefore his responsibility.

She licked her chafed lips. If he did find her in time there was a chance he might even forgive her and want their marriage to work. He'd probably agree Karma had punished her enough.

Her camel grunted as it sank to its front and back knees, Yasmine's head snapping at the motion so that she almost lost her seat. Her heart beat erratically, but she was too weak and dehydrated to fight. Instead she allowed one of Arif's men to drag her roughly off the saddle and inside the nearest tent.

His grasp was agonizing on her sunburned skin, but it didn't seem to matter to him. She wasn't just Arif's prisoner, she was white trash, garbage.

She was little more than a disposable commodity whose fragility was laughable at best. And her torture would no doubt begin sooner rather than later. The only small mercy was the relatively cool confines of the tent. They needn't torture her anymore in that regard; the sun had already done its damage.

The man shoved her so that she fell hard to the sandy floor. That he didn't even bother to truss her legs and arms together was a no-brainer. She had nowhere to go now except for the endless desert. "Water?" she asked weakly.

He laughed at her request and walked out.

*Asshole.*

She couldn't just sit and passively wait to die. She couldn't expect her husband, her proverbial knight in shining armor, to save her yet again.

*No. You saved your own ass the first time thanks to your ingenuity. You'll find a way to save yourself this time, too.*

First off, she needed water.

Then a weapon.

She staggered to her feet and looked around inside the tent. Going by the sacks of feed, possibly for the camels, and the dozen wooden crates that were pushed against the far wall, this tent was clearly used for storage.

Her pulse jerked. Was it possible water was stored in one of the crates?

A fire crackled to life outside, followed soon after by the tantalizing waft of cooked meat. She breathed deep, her belly rumbling and clenching. But though hunger pulled at her insides, she needed hydration first and foremost.

One of the men outside laughed, and a few others joined in. They sounded rowdy and jovial, and were likely drinking.

*Shit.*

She didn't want to think what those same men might do to her with alcohol filling their bellies and burning through their veins. She only hoped Arif wanted to keep her torture for himself, not share her around first to his men.

Forcing her leg muscles to cooperate, she lurched over to the crates and pried the lid off the first one stacked on top of two others. One of her fingernails snapped down to her quick. She ignored the pain, even as another nail tore off into a ragged end and bled.

She finally got the lid off and peered inside. Blankets of different colors and patterns were folded inside. She gritted her teeth and resisted throwing the whole crate with the blankets inside onto the floor.

The next crate she finally managed to pry open revealed clay jugs stacked inside. Hope tore through her as she opened a couple of the jugs, only to find red wine and arrack inside them. Of course there was no water. She didn't know whether to laugh or cry.

That it *was* liquid had to count as something? She was too thirsty to be fussy. She pulled the cork free from yet another jug and tipped it to her mouth, glugging down the red wine even as it spilled from the corners of her mouth and dripped down her chin.

She moaned. Never had red wine tasted so damn good! That it burned its way down her empty stomach and caused her to stumble forward before she retched violently was a secondary problem.

She swiped at her mouth with the back of her hand and giggled. *Holy shit.* She was already a little drunk. But of course she was. An empty stomach and severe dehydration meant she needed little of the stuff to feel its effects.

She backed away from the contents on the sandy floor. She needed to pace herself, go slower. She swigged one more mouthful. If she did happen to die today, at least she mightn't feel as much pain.

*Don't think like that! You're a fighter, not a quitter. You got away from Arif once, you can do it again!*

Except the more she tried to think of a way out of the mess, the more she drank, and the rowdier the men became outside the tent.

The light was beginning to dwindle with a distinct chill settling in the air, relieving the heat of her sunburn ever so slightly. She grabbed a blanket from out of the crate anyway and wrapped it tightly around her before she sat in the far corner of the tent. It wouldn't shield her body from Arif but it'd obstruct his touch for a minute or two, if that was what he had planned for her.

A tread sounded outside the tent before the doorway's fabric was flipped aside, silhouetting Arif's portly figure. She cast bleary eyes his way and almost giggled. He looked like a caricature of a person. A pig. No, a warthog.

She gave into the laugh, and he scowled as his hard gaze took in her half-drunken state.

"You been stealing from me, bitch?" He stepped inside the tent, the fabric swishing shut behind him and bringing everything back into gloomy shadow.

She lifted the jug, red wine sloshing free. "You haven't exactly been hospitable. I had to help myself."

"Then you won't mind if I do the same."

She knew exactly what he meant, but a part of her wanted to pretend none of this was happening. She lifted the wine jug. "Sure. Have as much wine as you want."

"If I wanted wine I wouldn't be here with you." He took off his sandals, then his headgear and robe, and her heart missed a beat as he exposed his fat, hairy body that was all too apparent even in the shadows. His cock was as stubby as his body, thick and squat, and as gross as the gray thatch of hair it poked out from, his mostly bald head gleaming in what was left of the daylight.

She shuffled backward with the jug until the tent wall stopped her from going any further. "In that case, I *do* mind."

He stepped forward. "I don't care what you—"

*Squelch.*

The look of horror that crossed his face as he stepped in her little welcoming package of sick left her giggling so hysterically hard she was gasping for breath.

"Bitch!" he roared.

# Chapter Twenty-One

Jamal moved to edge of the helicopter's passenger seat and peered through the open door where air rushed through. He scowled as Yusef sprinted for his life below them, away from the twin mounds of sand in the dunes and toward the boat where he intended on making his escape.

"What the fuck was he doing in the dunes?" Jamal growled into the headset, though his mind already knew exactly what the bastard had been doing.

The pilot took his eyes off his instruments to glance down at the ground below. There was no mistaking the pair of horizontal shapes of sand from high in the air. The pilot nodded at the mounds. "It looks as though he was digging graves."

Jamal's throat convulsed as nausea threatened. *Fuck.* Was it possible his wife was already dead and buried? Was he already too late to save her?

*No.* He'd *feel* it if she was gone. She'd become a part of his life and he'd know it if that part was missing.

He glanced back at the bleeping screen on the tracking device, which revealed Yusef's getaway. Yasmine wasn't anywhere in sight so it stood to reason Yusef had taken her wedding and engagement rings.

*Asshole.*

"Land us on the beach," he commanded.

The pilot nodded, but said, "Yusef will likely already be in the boat by the time—"

"Then angle us in the air so that I have a clear shot," he interjected as he pulled free a gun. His pilot was right, Jamal's usual quick thinking deserting him thanks to his fears. "And keep it steady."

The pilot maneuvered the bird into place even as Jamal leaned out and aimed at his ex-security guard.

*Bang.*

Jamal's shot was true and he felt a small measure of satisfaction as Yusef fell to the ground, no doubt shrieking in agony thanks to one of his knees getting blown out. He was crippled now and wouldn't be going anywhere.

The pilot whistled into his headset. "I heard you were an expert marksman. That proves it."

Jamal wasn't in any mood for pleasantries, not with his wife still missing. But it wasn't the pilot's fault Jamal had let down his guard and Yasmine had paid the price. "The bastard took my wife," he growled. "He never stood a chance."

When the helicopter landed, Jamal got out, ducking low under the rotors as he stalked toward the man he'd once trusted with his own life along with his wife's.

*Big mistake.* One that wouldn't ever be repeated again.

Yusef was attempting to crawl toward his boat with his shattered leg dangling behind him, a trail of blood in his wake.

Jamal easily caught up to him and put a foot on the back of Yusef's injured leg. That the man already had a bloodied cloth tied around his hand gave Jamal a little more joy. He only hoped it'd been his wife who'd inflicted the pain. Yusef cried out in pain and fear, and Jamal asked, "Going somewhere?"

"Don't hurt me, I beg you. I'll do whatever you want, just don't—"

Jamal pushed harder. "Where is my wife?"

*"Argh!"* Yusef wasn't the tough guy now. "I-I don't know. Somewhere in the d-desert."

"Where exactly and who took her?"

"I-I don't know where exactly. But it was Sheikh Arif and h-his men who took her. They put her on one of their c-camels and headed into the desert."

Jamal's gut clenched. He'd gotten news of Arif's incensed reaction not even an hour after Yasmine had already been taken. By then Jamal was already arranging the flight to track her down. That he could no longer follow her thanks to his technology bringing him instead to Yusef made Jamal want to howl with rage.

But he wasn't going to stop looking until he found her.

He glanced along the beach. Even with the rotors stirring up the sand there was still some faint markings from the camels. If the wind kept at bay for a little longer there was a chance they could follow the tracks from the air. And though darkness would soon be upon them, the helicopter's spotlight should give them enough illumination.

Either way, he needed to go now.

But first...

"What are you doing with my wife's rings?"

"H-how did you know I had them?"

Jamal snorted. "One of my best friends planted a tracking chip in his wife's ring. Turned out it was sound advice after she was kidnapped and it saved her life."

Yusef moaned pitifully, his leg twisted in an unnatural angle. He pulled the rings out of his robe and placed them in Jamal's hand. "I should have known better than to betray you."

Jamal grimaced as he put the rings in his suit pocket. "Yes, you should have." The jewelry felt tainted now, touched by evil. He'd get them professionally cleaned. Or buy Yasmine new ones. It was the least she deserved. But first he had to find his wife and beg her for forgiveness.

He glanced back at the dunes. "Whose bodies did you bury?"

"They w-were the other t-two kidnappers. Arif sh-shot them."

As much as Jamal wanted to do the very same thing to the traitorous scumbag lying on the sand, Jamal instead put his gun away and pivoted away from him. Shooting Yusef was a mercy he didn't want to give. The bastard deserved to suffer, just like Yasmine was probably suffering right now.

Ignoring Yusef's shout not to leave him, Jamal broke into a run and climbed back into the helicopter. Grabbing hold of his headset, he ordered, "Follow the tracks in the sand."

# Chapter Twenty-Two

Yasmine wanted to lash out, wanted to kick and to punch the fat sheikh even before he wasted a water skin by cleaning off his soiled foot. Only when he threw the skin aside and shambled toward her did she realize she had everything to gain and nothing to lose by fighting him off.

Except her struggles only excited Arif and he was surprisingly strong when he finally grabbed hold of her and held her down. "Oh, I'm going to enjoy hurting you, slut," he wheezed.

She gagged at his putrid breath that was even heavier on the red wine and onions. She'd die before she'd surrender. Panting from exertion, it took everything she had to relax so that his grip eased and she twisted away, getting her arm free and reaching for the wine.

She looked back at him with a hard smile. "Not if I hurt you first."

His eyes popped wide open as he caught sight of the heavy clay jug in her hand. Before he could react, she used the last of her strength to slam the jug against his temple.

*Crack.*

*Oomph.*

Red wine sloshed to the ground as Arif fell on top of her, leaving her panicky and gasping for air. When she finally succeeded in rolling him over and freeing herself, she knew by his glassy eyes and utter stillness he was dead long before she put her fingers on his neck and felt for his pulse.

Nothing.

*Holy shit.* She'd actually killed him.

The tent spun slowly around her as emotion coursed through her. A lot of women would thank her for ending his evil life, but she didn't feel relieved. She didn't feel anything at all. Not when she knew with absolute certainty his men would kill her. But not before they raped and tortured her.

Retribution would be their only goal.

She pushed to her feet. It was getting dark outside. Was it possible to use the darkness as cover and find her way back to the ocean before Arif's men got to her first?

She stood and swayed, and fear skittered through her followed by sudden hopelessness. She was far too dehydrated. Unless she could steal a water skin or two and trudge through the desert sand without getting lost and walking around in aimless circles, she couldn't even consider it as an option.

*Better to die of thirst in the desert than to be beaten and raped to death.*

She spied the skin that Arif had thrown aside. It had no lid and lay on its side but there might just be a few drops left. She hurried to it and picked it up, tipping it to her lips. A dribble of water made it into her mouth and she savored the small amount before she swallowed it down her parched throat.

She closed her eyes. *Glorious.* Even that underwhelming amount of water revived her and leant her some strength. Inhaling deeply, she took a step toward the fabric doorway.

"*Sheikh Arif!*"

One of the men call out their leader's name, and Yasmine froze, her pulse thudding in her ears and every muscle in her body clenching somewhere between a fight and flight response.

*Thwop. Thwop. Thwop.*

"Incoming helicopter!" another man called from a distance.

She didn't move, though hope flashed through her like a grenade on steroids. Jamal was here to rescue her!

Seconds later a spotlight moved over her tent, lighting up the dark, just as one of Arif's men peeled aside the fabric door. "Sheikh Arif, we're under attack!" The man's eyes glinted under the spotlight as he stared at his leader lying dead on the ground. He looked at Yasmine with hate-filled eyes. "You—"

*Bang.*

He dropped dead in the doorway, a bloody hole in his head and his staring eyes vacant.

More shots rang out, some pinging on metal that had to be the helicopter. Camel's grunted and bellowed, clearly made anxious by the helicopter noise, the gunfire, the shouts and screams.

Yasmine bit her lip. She needed to get out of the tent before one of Arif's men decided to either kill her before she was rescued, or use her as a shield to save himself.

It wasn't until the spotlight moved away from the tent that she stepped over the dead man with a little shudder. It was something of a relief to get out into the cool night air, though she was more exposed outside and instinctively pressed her back to the tent.

The spotlight picked out two men racing toward the camels, likely so they could ride away into the night or perhaps calm the animals down. *Bang. Bang.* One of the men fell to the ground followed immediately by the other, while at least half a dozen other men around the campsite fired at the helicopter, the noise of their shots giving her a rough indication of where her enemies were hiding.

She dropped to the ground and crawled along the sand, away from the gunfire and the camels, as well as the flickering campfire that shone dully against the darkness. She aimed to get as far away from everyone as possible, at least until she was certain it was safe.

She had no idea how far she'd crawled or even how long it'd taken her, but the campfire was nothing more than a distant light source, the helicopter even more distant and the gunfire much more sporadic.

She was gasping for breath when she finally stopped and pressed one side of her face to the sand, then closed her eyes.

She just needed to rest for a moment.

# Chapter Twenty-Three

Jamal jumped out of the safety of the helicopter, and though he itched to use his flashlight and shout out his wife's name, there was no way of knowing if his enemies were now all dead. The last thing he wanted was to be an easy target.

He hadn't yet seen Arif or Yasmine, and his heartbeat raced while his limbs went weak. He ran low to the ground, scanning left and right, his eyes adjusting to the gloom and the minimal light emitted from a quarter moon and countless stars.

He headed to the most elegant tent, no doubt Arif's temporary residence. Jamal was swift but cautious as he approached the fabric doorway. There was no sound from within, but it didn't mean the tent was unoccupied. He cocked his gun and swished aside the fabric, jerking his body one way to make him a moving target and harder to hit.

The tent was empty, with only wine jugs, a thick floor mat, a scattering of cushions and a woven blanket to indicate it was indeed Sheikh Arif's.

"Son of a bitch," Jamal gritted furiously under his breath.

He checked two more tents. Both were empty. He stayed low as he approached the tent where he'd shot a man from the helicopter. His breath eased out at finding the same man lying dead in the tent's doorway. Shooting from the air, even with his skill and the aid of a spotlight, was unpredictable at best.

Stepping over the dead body, he crouched low and listened for any sound before he drew the fabric aside and again jerked one way. It wasn't necessary, this tent, too, was empty of life. Literally. He scanned the mess of crates, a couple of which had been opened, before his stare settled on Arif.

Jamal's lip curled at the dead man, whose hairy and obese body was on full display. Going by his blood-smeared temple and the jug of wine close-by, he'd likely been bashed in the head.

Had Yasmine killed him? Hope surged. But as he looked around the empty tent, dread followed hot on its heels. She was nowhere to be seen. Coldness settled in the pit of his stomach, a sour taste filling his mouth. Had Arif raped her before she'd killed him?

His stomach rolled and he rocked back on his heels, his hands trembling.

*Hold it together. Yasmine needs you.*

Leaving the tent, he raced back to the helicopter and climbed inside. "Get us back into the air and circle the camp with the spotlight. My wife is still missing."

The pilot pulled them up into the air, the spotlight dazzling with its intensity as it lit up a circular patch of the desert beneath.

They ignored the bodies of the men who lay scattered around the camp, the helicopter and its spotlight covering an ever-expanding area in an effort to find Jamal's wife.

His heart wrenched. If he'd been wrong and Yasmine was dead he'd die himself. Life without her in it would be untenable. Unimaginable.

*I love her.*

His vision blurred and he couldn't see anything for a moment beyond his grief. How had he stuffed things up so badly? Bad enough he'd questioned her for sending money to her dad. After all, Jamal had given her free rein to spend it how she wanted and that was exactly what she'd done. That he'd been angry at her father for using her was a secondary problem, one he should have addressed with Zameer.

He exhaled heavily. He'd never forget the look of horror on her face when he'd told her about her father's gambling addiction and the real reason her dad had demanded such a large sum of money. The truth had hit her like a truck. But instead of comforting her like a loving husband, he'd taken her to bed for sex.

Even worse was that he'd pressured Yasmine into having a family, then raged at her for taking birth control pills and not wanting to be a mother. For fuck's sake, she was all of twenty years of age. Of course she didn't yet want to have a baby.

He dragged a hand over his face. He'd been an arrogant fool and Yasmine deserved better. If she ever forgave him it'd be a miracle.

"Is that the Sheikha?"

The pilot's voice snapped Jamal out of his misery and regret. He peered at the parcel of desert lit up below, recognizing Yasmine's inert form immediately. His throat dried, making his voice raspy. "That's her. Get us to the ground."

It seemed forever but would have only been minutes before the helicopter landed. Jamal jumped out and ran toward his wife, dropping to his knees and turning her onto her back. Her face was a mess of bruises and swelling, her blonde hair limp and stained with blood. His heart wrenched. "Yasmine, are you hurt? Talk to me!"

Her lashes flickering apart, she croaked, "Please tell me you shot all those men?"

Relief flooded through him. "Yes, I did. They can't hurt you anymore."

"Good." She smiled weakly. "I knew you'd come for me."

Her words both riddled him further with guilt and sparked his love for her even deeper. He didn't deserve her gratitude.

"I think I like this uncivilized side you warned me about," she added softly.

His heart twisted in his chest. He'd raze the world to the ground if needed to make it up to her.

# Chapter Twenty-Four

Yasmine was only half-aware of being lifted in Jamal's powerful arms. She was too lost in his sandalwood and cinnamon scent, and the sense of calmness that followed. Even with his urgent, clipped instructions to someone her whole body was blessedly numb as she slumped against him, her emotions hazy.

Everything felt like an out-of-body experience, from the jostling motion as he climbed up into a seat and held her protectively against him, to the helicopter rotors roaring before they were lifted into the air.

He held a bottle to her lips and as cool water slipped past her dry lips and down her parched throat, she gulped at it greedily.

"Just a little bit for now."

"Thank you," she managed weakly, before her lashes fluttered closed and darkness spirited her away.

She woke to sunlight flooding her eyelids and a strong awareness of Jamal sitting beside her bed, his hand clasping hers. She kept her eyes closed for a little longer, savoring the feeling of being safe once again, of no longer being on high alert.

Although the war zone was behind her, she couldn't help but wonder if she had a new battle on her hands. One that involved her begging her husband to stay with her and work things out.

"You're awake."

She opened her eyes and cracked a smile, though her pulse thudded dully in her ears at seeing the dark circles under his eyes, his hollow cheeks and the deep weariness emanating from him.

She swallowed hard. Even at his most vulnerable he was a beautiful male. He probably didn't look a fraction as bad as she did. She blinked.

At least her eye swelling seemed to have gone down. She could see more clearly now. She touched her lip. *Ouch.*

"You have scrapes and bruises everywhere. Not to mention serious sunburn." He exhaled roughly. "I had my personal physician examine and treat you while you slept. He said your body will recover fully by the week with lots of R&R."

She nodded, while her mind sent her horrid flashbacks of Arif holding her down. "I'm sure I'll be as good as new," she said drily.

Jamal's mouth thinned a little. Had he somehow sensed the disturbing images in her mind? Or perhaps he hadn't yet told her everything?

She blinked. "What else did your physician say?"

"He said that although you had many bruises, you weren't touched intimately."

She gaped. "You had your doctor examine me down there?"

Jamal frown. "Of course. I had to know how hurt you were and how far Arif had gone—"

"In case you needed to dump me faster than a hot coal?" she interrupted bitterly.

He flinched, the color draining from his face. And though his eyes held hers, his distress was all too clear. "No, so that I could run further tests and organize a counsellor to help you get through your ordeal."

"Why would you do that?"

"You're my wife, angel."

"Let's be honest," she said bitterly. "All you want from me—all you ever wanted—was for me to give you children."

"Yasmine, no. I—"

"You said it yourself." And the pain of that knowledge hurt far more than her recent physical and mental trauma. Who knew a broken heart could hurt so damn much? "You want me to give you children so that they share our royal bloodline."

He shook his head. "If that was true and your lineage was all I wanted we wouldn't be married now."

A rush of foreboding swept through her, her voice sharp. "What exactly do you mean by that?"

He sighed heavily. "Forget I said anything. You need to rest. The doctor will be here again soon."

"I won't rest until you tell me the truth." She held his eyes. "Please. I don't want any more lies between us."

He gently brushed back her hair, like she was breakable porcelain. "Neither do I, angel. But we'll speak once you're feeling better."

She shook her head as an inkling of an idea formed inside her muzzy head, taunting her with its unlikelihood as well as its possibility. "No." Her vision misted. "I need to know now." She clasped his hand. "Is Sheikh Zameer my biological father?"

Jamal squeezed his eyes shut, as though shutting her out would also shut down the truth.

"He's not, is he?" she asked flatly.

"Zameer is infertile and unable to produce children," Jamal conceded gently.

Shock made her want to sit up and demand a thousand answers, but fatigue was also rolling through her in waves, the effort of talking using up the last of her strength. "Then who is my father?"

"He was one of your mother's bodyguards."

"*Was?*"

"He died in a street brawl just a couple of months after you were born."

"How do you know so much?"

"I only found out myself a few hours ago." He pushed a hand over his face. "I hired a PI who was able to dig up the information I needed fast."

Grief for her real father—a man she'd never know—threatened to swallow her whole, while the knowledge her mother had an affair with another man left her whole world tilted and off-balance. Yet paradoxically, everything else fell into place like pieces of a puzzle. "At least now I know why Zameer never loved me. I was living proof of his failure to produce heirs."

"If it's any comfort, I believe he's proud of the daughter he raised, despite the fact you aren't of his blood."

Zameer's words echoed in her head. *You've become more like me than I realized.*

"I'm nothing like him."

"No, you're not. You're good and kind, and you're beautiful inside and out."

She swallowed hard. "Please don't pretend to care about me. Not anymore."

His hand tightened around hers. "Yasmine, I *do* care. I love you. I think I loved you from the very first moment I saw you in my bed, like an angel from heaven."

Hope warmed her heart, grief subsiding as love surged for him in return. "You do?"

He held her gaze, his smile soft, tender. "I've never been more certain about anything or anyone in my life."

All her fears and insecurities seemed to melt away, right along with her recent trauma. "You don't know how much that means to me," she said, voice trembling. Her vision misted. "I love you, too."

He inhaled sharply. "You're not just saying that?"

"I mean every word." She lifted one of her bandaged hands and touched his face. "We really do belong together."

"Always and forever. You are mine," he said hoarsely. "My angel."

Despite the adrenaline hit, everything was starting to get fuzzy around the edges, with sleep beckoning. It took every ounce of willpower to push back fatigue and ask, "But what about children?"

"We'll have them...one day. When we're both ready."

A smile tugged at the corner of her lips. "You really mean that, don't you?"

"I was a fool to allow my past to affect our future."

"Your past?"

His breath whistled between his teeth. "I lost a baby...a stillborn boy."

Another surge of adrenaline for a moment pushed away bone-deep weariness. "I'm so sorry."

"I'm the one who is sorry." A sad smile twisted his lips. "I should never have expected you to want children with me. You're still so young, as Sheikha you have enough responsibilities."

She didn't have the energy to reassure him that being Sheikha was child's play to her now. She had other, more significant topics of conversation to address. "What happened to the mother of your child?"

"You don't have to worry about her," he said gently. "She has her own life now, with an allowance to sustain her for life."

Yasmine had a sneaking suspicion it wasn't quite that simple, but she was even more aware they could handle whatever came their way from now on. She wasn't trapped living with Jamal, she was liberated. Jamal would encourage her to do whatever she wanted.

And oh, how she wanted. Not just him, but children, too. And she'd put her degrees to good use.

But first, she needed to rest. She had the rest of her life to love her husband and to live life to its fullest.

# Epilogue

*Three months later...*

The ballroom was alive with music, but not with the orchestral sounds one might expect. A famous popstar was on stage with backing vocalists and a fabulous band, while guests danced on the black-and-white tiled floor around Yasmine and Jamal like they were chess pieces on a board.

"Happy birthday, Yasmine!"

Yasmine spun in Jamal's arms and smiled at the gorgeous, dark-haired woman who held the title of "mistress" to Sheikh Fayez. That Fayez appeared to be as smitten with Jazmina as any husband would be to his wife was the understatement of the century. Even now the two of them were dancing cheek-to-cheek.

Jazmina might also hold the title of most stunning woman in the room, if not for the fact Jamal's stare constantly hovered on Yasmine, as though she was the only woman in the world for him. It clearly mattered little to him that her birthright didn't officially make her a sheikha.

Perhaps though Jazmina's pedigree mattered to Fayez?

Yasmine smiled. "Thanks Jazmina. I hope you're enjoying the party."

Jazmina threw her head back and laughed, just as Fayez stepped back and spun her around with one hand. "Best party ever!"

Jamal chuckled along with Fayez, both men enjoying the radiant delight Jazmina exuded.

Yasmine's smile widened as she watched the two lovebirds together. "You really do make the most gorgeous couple."

Fayez winked. "Have you and Jamal looked in the mirror lately?"

Yasmine fluttered her lashes with over-exaggerated mirth. "Oh, stop!"

Jamal grinned at the couple. "You might want to make it official soon, Fayez, before some other man whisks her away and you lose her forever."

Jazmina's smile faded, and Fayez stiffened before he swung her away from them, then bent to murmur something in her ear.

Yasmine winced as she looked up at Jamal. "That didn't go down very well."

Jamal nodded. "I can't fathom Fayez's reluctance, he clearly adores her."

The pop singer began a slow ballad and Yasmine wound her arms around Jamal's neck. "I'm sure they'll work it out."

She only wished her mother and Zameer would do the same thing. But Yasmine had discovered her mother was still in mourning for a dead man—Yasmine's biological dad—and that although Zameer was actually deeply in love with Valentina, she didn't return his feelings. He'd taken comfort in the many women at his disposal in the harem, while seeking consolation with his gambling.

It had opened Yasmine's blinkered eyes and made her realize how quickly she'd been judge and jury. She didn't blame either one of them for their feelings or their actions. She knew firsthand that one couldn't simply turn off emotions like a light switch.

She only hoped Zameer really was getting help for his gambling addiction like he'd promised.

Jamal looked down at her, his eyes glittering with approval while his hands tightened on her ass. She wore a simple, fitted black dress that contrasted with her blonde hair, and yet she'd never felt more beautiful or cherished.

Since her kidnapping, Jamal had been extra attentive, even cancelling events just to be with her until she felt emotionally strong enough to go with him to business functions and social gatherings. Having his strength and support had sped up her inner healing. He'd been her rock, her lover and her friend.

She worshipped him.

But how would he react when she told him the truth? She hadn't gone back on her birth control pills, had even presumed she'd be lucky to fall pregnant after the turmoil she'd gone through. Now here she was two months pregnant and just shy of beginning to show.

Sheikh Mahindar and his wife Arabelle, floated past them with their gazes locked on one another. Yasmine couldn't help but admire Arabelle's svelte figure, though she'd only recently had a baby girl. Mahindar certainly seemed to be devoted to her, but then Yasmine had no doubt he'd feel the same way about his wife no matter if she was pudgy or slim.

Jamal glanced at Mahindar and Arabelle, before he turned back to Yasmine. "Everything okay?"

She nodded. "I was just thinking how happy they look even after having a baby."

"A baby was never going to make them love one another any less."

You stared up at him. "Do you think it made them fall for one another even harder?"

He blinked, his face turning serious. "If what you're really asking is am I happy without you wanting kids, then yes, angel, I am. You're my sun and my stars. We've got all the time we need to have a family and—"

"I'm pregnant."

He froze, and she followed suit, both of them standing like statues while everyone around them danced and jostled past. His eyes glittering, he croaked, "You're not just saying that?"

She bit her bottom lip. "No. It's true, Jamal. I haven't taken birth control pills since you brought me back home. We're having a baby."

He whooped so loud everyone on the dance floor paused, their stares landing on Jamal and Yasmine. Leaning down and kissing her soundly, he released her to run through the crowd and toward the popstar, grabbing the microphone from her with a muttered apology.

The band stopped playing and Jamal's gaze held Yasmine's as he spoke into the microphone. "Everyone, I have an announcement to make." A hush filled the ballroom before his voice rang out again. "As you know it's not my birthday, it's my beautiful wife's. But it turns out Yasmine's given *me* the best present in the world." At the continued silence, he proclaimed loudly, "We're having a baby!"

# Chapter One of The Sheikh's Secret Mistress

Jazmina Fadel stared into the mirror, indifferent to her stunning good looks. Once upon a time she'd felt blessed by what she'd been gifted, now she almost resented her full lips with their bright red lipstick, her inky-black hair with its natural waves, and her unusual violet eyes that revealed a heritage that wasn't all Middle Eastern.

How would her lover Sheikh Fayez react if she blotted off her lipstick and the mascara that highlighted her best features? She stepped back to look critically at her lilac evening gown that clung to her slender curves and accentuated her eyes. What would he say if she opened the door to him wearing a shapeless black burqa?

Because clearly her beauty was all he cared about since he wasn't making any plans to further their relationship.

How had the first six months of their relationship hit such dizzying heights when the next six had hit so many lows? She'd been thrilled when she'd caught Fayez's attention, been on top of the world when their one night together had turned into four more before he'd surprised her with a two bedroom luxury condo complete with a closet full of clothes.

She exhaled softly, her eyes luminescent under the downlights. Tonight was their twelve month anniversary and her last hope that he'd take their relationship to the next level.

*Just because three of his closest friends have married the love of their lives, it doesn't mean he'll do the same.*

He seemed all too happy with their present arrangement. And why wouldn't he be? As his mistress she gave him exclusive rights to her body...to her soul.

*Knock. Knock. Knock.*

She started at the sound. Though Fayez had purchased the condo he respected her privacy and never walked in without her permission. That she longed for him to do just that burned a hole in her chest.

*Pfft.* She was so desperate for a normal relationship it bordered on tragic.

Every woman she knew wanted the fairytale prince, and she hadn't been any different. Now all she wanted was a regular man who'd want to commit. And therein lay the problem. It didn't matter what he wanted, it only mattered what his people wanted. She had no pedigree. She wasn't a princess or a sheikha. And Fayez's people expected him to marry royalty, not a commoner mistress.

How many times had his name recently been linked with Princess Takima?

Her throat tightening painfully, she pasted a smile on her face and grabbed her clutch purse before she stalked out of her bathroom and through the lounge room. She didn't even bother to glance at her gorgeous kitchen. She loved to bake, and recently she'd begun baking cookies and cakes for those homeless and less fortunate.

It was her little secret. Fayez wanted her wrapped in cotton wool at all times and undoubtedly believed she spent her days having facials while enjoying pedicures and manicures. He'd have no idea she knew her way around the kitchen.

He might lead a busy life, but he rarely stayed in with her other than to take her to bed. Instead he took her out for dinners and lunches, and occasionally to parties and events, presumably to show her off like one did a high class escort.

*You're his mistress. You're no better than a whore. The only difference is that you don't share your body with other men and you get a house and clothes along with the money.*

Fayez wasn't too proud to admit he enjoyed the best of everything. His private residences, his fleet of rare cars, his Arabian racehorses, his many businesses.

*His mistress.*

Her lungs constricted, spots for a moment dancing in her vision. Why did it hurt so much that he adored her good looks? It should make her happy, but what was the point of it all if he didn't also appreciate her inner beauty?

She shook her head, her fake smile faltering. He deserved his success. He worked hard and played harder. That she was his plaything never ceased to equally amaze and alarm her. He might be fixated on her for now but how much longer could she reasonably expect it to last?

She scraped a hand through the waves of her loose hair. She had to stop thinking about the future and instead live in the moment. She'd always dressed and acted the part of flawless and picture-perfect mistress for the great and renowned Sheikh of Abnia, and she wasn't about to stop now.

She opened the door and her breath caught as Fayez stood waiting for her in a charcoal gray, tailored suit. She swallowed hard. No matter if he wore a thobe or western clothes he was gorgeous, his style as effortless as his business acumen.

He smiled, his glittering dark eyes sweeping over her in quick appraisal. "Gorgeous as always, Jazmina."

She managed a smile in return, and she lifted her head for the slow and tender kiss he always bestowed on her before they faced the outside world together. The slow, lingering kiss in the foyer's elevator as it then swept them to the ground floor was also a routine that she enjoyed far too much. Perhaps because it took her mind off her doubts as much as it reminded her their passion hadn't died.

They truly were good together.

He pulled back and nuzzled her ear, his voice husky as he murmured, "I'm so tempted to take you right here, right now."

A shaft of need pulsed through her and she tipped her head back as he pressed heated kisses along her throat, intoxicating her further. Dear Lord, he was a drug and she was an addict, wanting more of him despite a future without him in it.

She was still reeling and all but propped up by the powerful strength of his arm when they stepped out of the elevator. Cameras immediately flashed and Fayez stiffened even as he managed a smile while shielding her from the media as he escorted her out of the foyer and its glass fronted doors, then into the back of a dark sedan.

It wasn't until their driver merged the sedan into the traffic that Fayez growled through his teeth. "I can't have reporters just showing up in the same building where you live. They're like vultures waiting for prey. I'll beef up security and—"

"No." She shook her head. "No security, please. It will only attract more attention."

"Jaz, I can't risk—"

"I can take care of myself." She didn't need to tell him she'd been doing it long before she'd met him, scarcely more than a girl on the verge of womanhood with everything against her except for her looks. "I always said I wanted to live a normal life outside of yours. Only when I'm with you do I accept that normal isn't ever going to be an option."

He winced, then nodded and said, "I understand."

So why did the hard line of his jaw tell her that he wasn't going to yield to her? She clasped one side of his face, the bristles of his beard scratchy yet soft. She loved touching him. "Do you?" she asked softly.

He looked at her, his eyes pained. Then he blinked and all trace of emotion was gone. "I just...don't want to see you hurt."

She bit back a sharp laugh. It was a little too late for that. Oh, she might be happy now, but her heart would be crushed the moment he chose to walk away and move onto someone else.

"I'll be fine," she lied, smiling at him before she reached up to kiss him.

He groaned into her mouth, and she slipped the tip of her tongue between his full, sexy lips, tasting the faint undertones of premium whiskey as he deepened the kiss with a rumbling growl.

Her heart gave a sudden wrench. God, she was going to miss kissing him, almost as much as she was going to miss him sliding his hands up and down her body while he thrust his hips forward and his hard cock filled her.

The car slowed and pulled over, the restaurant they often frequented coming in to view. He drew back, his dark eyes snaring hers. "Do you have any idea what you do to me?"

She grinned saucily and nodded at the bulge in his pants. "I have a fair idea."

It was, after all, why she was with him. And why he kept her. Their passion was explosive, addicting, but the moment that passion dried up, if not before, was the moment he'd leave.

*Unless he proposes tonight.*

The insidious whisper filled her with hope. Who knew what might happen on their first year anniversary? Fayez was his own man. He didn't need to heed his advisors wishes, or listen to his people for that matter, not when it came to marriage.

She was a little less anxious when they approached their favorite, intimate table, where Fayez pulled out her chair and she sat with a smile of thanks. She loved that though he was a sheikh, he was also a gentleman. A powerful and ruthless man whose gentler side captivated her, making her want him all the more.

A drinks waiter approached and Fayez smiled at Jazmina and asked, "The usual?"

She nodded. "Yes, please."

Fayez ordered a bottle of the crisp, fruity champagne she enjoyed. Whether he enjoyed it or not was another matter, but he always shared it with her.

A blonde woman, perhaps a decade older than Jazmina's twenty years, walked toward them then, her outfit screaming haute couture along with her expensive scent. She stopped and spoke to Fayez, her body oozing sex appeal and her unsubtle interest stirring something tart and acidic deep inside Jazmina's chest.

Her breath hitched. Was this the woman who'd be her replacement?

As if reading her mind, the blonde arched a brow Jazmina's way. "I'm sorry, I don't believe we've met?" she purred.

Fayez's hand clenched his napkin, but his introduction was smooth, unhurried. "Daphne meet Jazmina, my...date. Jazmina, Daphne is an old friend of the family."

Daphne's laugh tinkled. "Oh, I think I was a little more than that, Sheikh Fayez." She touched his shoulder in a familiar caress, her sparkling, cat-green eyes for a moment holding Jazmina's. "It's so lovely to meet you, Jazmina. But please, don't let me interrupt your date."

"We won't," Jazmina said coolly.

Fayez didn't appear to notice when the blonde sashayed away, he was too busy assessing Jazmina. "Are you okay?"

Resentment flared. Whatever Daphne had been to Fayez it was well and truly over now, even if Daphne still held a candle for him. Her throat dried. Was that how Jazmina would be classified in the future? A passing acquaintance? A woman he used to fuck?

That she'd still be nobody and nothing if it wasn't for him made her resentment fester more. She lifted her chin, her lie a brazen one. "Of course. Why wouldn't I be okay?"

The drinks waiter returned and poured them each a glass of champagne before he placed the bottle into an ice bucket and retreated.

"Daphne means nothing to me," Fayez said, as though he'd read Jazmina's mind.

As though she wasn't about to fall apart at the seams.

"I kind of gathered that," she gritted.

He cocked his head to the side. "What is going on with you tonight? You haven't been yourself from the moment I picked you up."

A tidal wave of emotion swept over her, cracking her open. "I *am* myself," she retorted. "And maybe *that* is the problem. I'm good enough between the sheets, but I'll never be anything more to you, will I?"

His face flashed with shock. "How can you say that?"

"How can I not?" She stood. "This was just going to be another dinner, wasn't it?" At his frown she added, *"Whatever.* I'm no longer hungry. I'll find my own way home."

For your exclusive FREE story: Her Dark Guardian, and where you can find out when my next book is available, as well as other news, cover reveals and more, sign up for my newsletter: https://madmimi.com/signups/121695/join

Check out my website – http://www.melteshco.com/

You can also friend me on Facebook at https://www.facebook.com/mel.teshco

Or my author Facebook page at https://www.facebook.com/MelTeshcoAuthor

And occasionally on Twitter at https://twitter.com/melteshco

Contact me: melteshco@yahoo.com.au

If you enjoy my books I'd be delighted if you would consider leaving a review. This will help other readers find my books ☺

## About the Author

Mel Teshco loves to write scorching hot sci-fi and contemporary stories with an occasional paranormal thrown into the mix. Not easy with seven cats, two dogs and a fat black thoroughbred vying for attention, especially when Mel's also busily stuffing around on Facebook. With only one daughter now living at home to feed two minute noodles, she still shakes her head at how she managed to write with three daughters and three stepchildren living under the same roof. Not to mention Mr. Semi-Patient (the one and same husband hoping for early retirement...he's been waiting a few years now.) Clearly anything is possible, even in the real world.

*Want more Mel Teshco books?*

**Contemporary:**
*Desert Kings Alliance: series order*
The Sheikh's Runaway Bride (book 1)
The Sheikh's Captive Lover (book 2)
The Sheikh's Forbidden Wife (book 3)
The Sheikh's Secret Mistress (book 4)
The Sheikh's Defiant Princess (book 5)
*The VIP Desire Agency: series order*
Lady in Red (book 1)
High Class (book 2)
Exclusive (book 3)
Liberated (book 4)
Uninhibited (book 5)
The VIP Desire Agency Boxed Set (all 5 books in the series)
*Box sets with authors Christina Phillips & Cathleen Ross*
Sheikhs & Billionaires
Taken by the Sheikh
Taken by the Billionaire
Taken by the Desert Sheikh
Resisting the Firefighter
*Standalone longer length titles: (50k-100k)*
Highest Bid
As I Am
*Standalone novellas and short stories: (15k-40K)*
Stripped
Clarissa
Camilla
Selena's Bodyguard (also part of the Christmas Assortment Box)\
*Anthologies:*
Down and Dusty: The Complete Collection
The Christmas Assortment Box

Secret Confessions: Sydney Housewives
**Science Fiction:**
*The Virgin Hunt Games:*
The Virgin Hunt Games volume 1
The Virgin Hunt Games volume 2
The Virgin Hunt Games volume 3
*Coming soon*
The Virgin Hunt Games volumes 4-6
*Dragons of Riddich: series order:*
Kadin (prequel - book 1)
Asher (book 2)
Baron (book 3)
Dahlia (book 4)
Wyatt (book 5)
Valor (book 6)
The Queen (book 7)
*Alien Hunger: series order*
Galactic Burn (book 1)
Galactic Inferno (book 2)
Galactic Flame (book 3)
*Coming soon*
Galactic Blaze (book 4)
*Nightmix: series order:*
Lusting the Enemy (book 1)
Abducting the Princess (book 2)
Seducing the Huntress (book 3)
*Winged & Dangerous: series order*
Stone Cold Lover (book 1)
Ice Cold Lover (book 2)
Red Hot Lover (book 3)
Winged & Dangerous Box Set (all 3 books in the series)

*Dirty Sexy Space continuity with authors Shona Husk and Denise Rossetti:*
Yours to Uncover (book 1)
Mine to Serve (book 6)
Ours to Share (book 8)
*Awakenings series with Kylie Sheaffe*
No Ordinary Gift (book 1)
Believe (book 2)
Homecoming (book 3)
*Standalone longer length titles: (50k-100k)*
Dimensional
Mutant Unveiled
Shadow Hunter
Existence
*Standalone novellas and short stories: (15k-40K)*
Identity Shift
Moon Thrall
Blood Chance
Carnal Moon
*And coming soon in 2023:*
*Alien Fugitives: series order*
Nero (book 1) *pre-order*
Jasper (book 2)
Sienna (book 3)

Lightning Source UK Ltd.
Milton Keynes UK
UKHW010933060223
416537UK00002B/537